ADRIFT IN SKINNY WATER

CHAD BOLES

Adrift in Skinny Water
Published by
Canary Media, LLC
Atlanta, GA

For my wife, to whom
I am eternally grateful,
and to my dearest friends
for editorial improvement.

Other books by Chad Boles
Blinded Authority

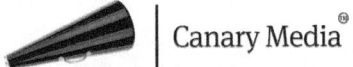 Canary Media®

CONTENTS

SHARK REPELLANT

Toby raced his truck down the long county road leading to the beach. The October dusk cast shadows over the pine trees as the sun's last effort beamed through the needle tops. The pine trees were held back by a high fence bordering the shoulders of the road. The fence separated the hunters from the undisturbed wildlife, and the wildlife from the gauntlet of highway death. The result was a 30-mile-long drag strip.

Toby Durante was the child prodigy of his racing legend father. He was taking Gunner Ellis on a fishing adventure. The local hot rod dealer, Mike's Speed Shop, encouraged it in hopes of putting Gunner's face on a billboard advertisement. It didn't hurt that Toby's Durante Machine Shop built the engines for Mike's. Gunner was the star quarterback for the Pirates, pride of the maroon and black and no stranger to the receiving end of gifts and handouts.

The turbo charger in Toby's truck, hidden under a hump in the hood, whiffled to a slow whir as he backed off the pedal. He drifted to a stop next to the gas pumps. The truck sat under the fluorescent lights of a gas station—this the only store for miles between town and the beach.

Toby pumped gas while Gunner went inside to buy bait. Whole frozen bonita full of blood were no good to eat, but the smell drew sharks for miles. It was Saturday night in coastal country, and the boys were loaded for bear—or, well, sharks.

Toby's head was covered in rusty brown hair and his brown eyes held the familiar friendliness of the region. Fourth generation Durante, he couldn't be more local. His hard bottom racing shoes were a must for this trip. Born to speed in his dad's engine shop, he had zero interest in chasing girls or team sports. Not that the co-eds in town didn't have any interest, but the time required for a catch was added directly on top of his track times.

While pumping gas, he rested his hand on the truck bed and inspected the gear, ensuring all the equipment was strapped down for the wild ride Gunner had in store. He looked over the two shark rigs in the bed. They sat next to the cooler, the width of the bed and strapped against the cab. The rigs were composed of two massive barrels of fishing line, weed eater string thick, mounted on six-foot rods, themselves the diameter of hammer handles. The line looped through the top rod-eyes. Both of the talon hooks cinched into machined holes on the reels, keeping the line tight against the rods. Held next to one of the bed's wheel wells was a surf board.

Toby was Gunner's one night fishing guide and outfitter. In a few months, Gunner would be gone, but not too far away; up the road playing for State U. Gunner was tall, taught and swarthy. He swaggered in flip flops from the front door of the store holding a bag containing two six packs. He gestured to a girl, Melanie, walking behind him and dragging two dead fish.

Melanie wore the radiant spark of rural beauty. Her silky skin glistened from the fall sun. Her long hair fell around the straps of her tank top. Her brown legs came all the way up to her frayed denim shorts struggling to stay on her hips.

Toby tried hiding the grease under his fingernails by putting his hands in the pockets of his dry-fit board shorts, but couldn't squander a chance to show her a little chivalry. He ran around the truck and grabbed the two fish out of her hands. He tossed them in the cooler and then eyed her with the casual glance of a life-long friendship. "Sorry about that, Melanie. Gunner doesn't carry his own bags." Then to the football star, "Dipshit."

"What," Gunner dismissed. "I got beer, didn't I?'

"You got a hole in your head is what you got. I'm driving a race car. Plus, if Melanie went to school in town, she'd be the homecoming queen not your personal valet."

"Aww, thank you, Toby," she said, standing near Gunner, obviously attracted to his quarterback aura.

"You're my homecoming queen, aren't ya' babe?" Gunner responded. Then he winked at Toby. He threw one six pack in the cab and the other in the cooler next to the frozen bonita. Toby put the nozzle back in the pump and said to Melanie with light hearted concern, "Gus let you work out here all by yourself?"

"Dad's working the other store and momma's around the corner at the house. I can handle strangers that don't know what's what." Snatching the bottom of her loose tank top hem, she exposed a concealed carry pistol. "You want to take a shot at the title, Toby? I know you. You aren't as tough as all those pretty girls in town think you are," she said, her smile outshining the fluorescent beams overhead.

Toby threw his hands up and shook his head. "No, thanks, miss," and hopped in the truck.

Gunner looked at Toby, unsure if he was kidding. Then he kissed Melanie on the lips. "I'd come back by later, but you'll be closed."

"Don't bring those smelly sharks around here, Toby," she said, turning to follow another customer back into the store.

Charging the turbo up to a loud spinning whirr, Toby alerted Gunner without looking at him, "Buckle up. We're hammer down from here to the beach." He released the brake and the screeching tires launched them to full speed. In the lengthening shadows, the headlights bled out onto the pavement. Separating the strip of the road, the dashed yellow lines became one. The speedometer was pinned to the peg making the truck's true speed unknown. Toby only let up just slightly for a caution light. Gunner sipped a beer bubbling from the can top and yelled over the roar of the engine, "What's in this thing?'

"A turbocharger pushing an LS motor to twice the horsepower. About 750, if you're buying?"

"No thanks," he said, and swallowed beer that poured out around his mouth. "You're not worried about cops?"

"Nah. Pops and I build all their engines," Toby yelled. Changing the subject to some business he said, "Y'know, Mike's Speed Shop would love to pay you to put your mug on a billboard."

"Sure. Huck's Furniture and Gun Shop paid me all

summer to sit in their two best recliners on the showroom floor."

Toby's truck blasted through a few more miles in mere minutes. "So, how many girlfriends you have?" he asked, his two hands gripping the wheel and his eyes set dead ahead.

"I dunno," Gunner replied nervously. With one hand he was squeezing his beer can and with the other he was leaving finger dents in the door handle. "Depends on the week. Including Melanie, maybe three. But she's getting close to being my starter. We'll see how much she wants it," he explained, swilling the rest of his beer. He crumpled the empty can and dropped in the rattling floorboard, "It'll be alright. I like her."

"Make sure and throw those things out when we get to the beach. This truck is barely legal as it is," Toby warned.

"Sh-Sure," Gunner said, vibrating from the speed.

"I'm serious. The sheriff deputies know me, but drinking beer on the road will land us both in lock-up."

Arriving in time for sunset, Toby pulled off the road and into a parking lot. Old tire ruts in the nearby sand marked off road adventure. "Hang on. This is where it gets real."

"What do you call the trip here?" Gunner asked with a whimper.

Toby spun up the turbocharger again. The truck sailed into the sun and over the top of a couple of dunes, sand spewing behind them as the front wheels lifted off the ground. Landing near the water's edge, he shut down the motor on a remote spot of beach. He looked to Gunner and asked, "How'd you like that?"

Gunner removed his death grip from the console and the door handle. "Go Pirates! Arrrrgggh!" he said in his best Blackbeard impression. "I didn't know you hicks were out here doing this stuff."

Toby tried not to react to Gunner's choice of words. "Got to keep busy doing something. None of us play sports," he replied casually.

Wiggling his fingers, Gunner cracked another beer. "Want one?" he asked.

"Sure." Toby snapped the top open. Then he changed the subject. "Have you and Melanie, um, done it?"

"No. But I'll let you know soon as we do, since you're interested."

Toby shrugged. "You better be careful you don't get shot. She shoots better than her old man, and he's already killed a trespasser." The warning hung in silence for a second.

They both got out of the truck, lugged the gear near the shore and set the rods. The harvest moon shone so bright, they didn't need flashlights. Hustling through the guide's work, Toby threaded the hook shanks through both of the bonita. He directed Gunner to unclick the bail so it free-spooled. The water was calm. He hopped on the board and paddled out past the second sand bar and dropped the bait. When he returned, he said to Gunner, "Your turn."

"Not me," said Gunner. "All that chum out there? They're counting on both my arms to throw touchdowns. I'm just looking out for my future."

Toby was soaking wet and shook his head. He made a judgment straight to Gunner's face: "What a wuss.' Then he repeated the same routine with the second rod.

Rubbing their asses in the sand to carve out a seat, they settled in for the wait. The duo allowed the dabbling surf and the slow tick-tick-tick of the expectant reels to hypnotize their conversation into a trusting back and forth.

They were illuminated by the moon, now directly overhead. Gunner gulped a swig of beer and spoke first. "Did Melanie's dad really kill somebody?"

"That's what my dad said. It was justified, though. A guy came in the store high on pills and waving a gun— But enough about that. You and the team are chalking up the wins pretty fast. Think you can go all the way to state again?'

"You can bet on it. The farther we go, the more money State U will pay me."

"Pay you?"

"Oh yeah. I know you hicks don't keep up, but colleges pay now."

"That so," Toby said, and sipped his beer.

"Yep. The bigger the college the more money."

Toby furled his brows. "You get any other offers besides State U?"

"Sure, but they're so far off. Denver State pays good, but University of Los Angeles pays the most. Their coach calls me every week."

"What's wrong with LA?"

"That's a long way from home," Gunner replied, sheepishly. "And I'm not going anywhere unless I can start as a freshman. So, wherever I go, I enroll right after Christmas. I have to learn the playbook before next season."

"Well, we may not know much out in the sticks, but we get movies on TV. There're some smokin' hot women in LA."

"I know."

"And we get football games, too. The quarterback at ULA stinks. You can outrun him and outthrow him."

The lines on the reel interrupted as they began tick-tick-ticking with the falling tide. "Is that a bite?" Gunner asked.

"Maybe," Toby said. "Give it a bit. When they take it, they're gone. The reel will scream. You'll know," he said, letting the conversation fall off for a moment.

The breeze began to pick up and Toby started back in, "Think you can get a commercial at State U?"

"For what? Camo hunting gear and alligator skinned boots?"

"Just asking. I don't know anything about it."

"Maybe in LA. That's what the coach said anyway," Gunner said.

Toby imagined Gunner's opportunities. "What the hell, Gunner? You could learn to surf. Commercials. Money. Be on TV every Saturday. State U is only on that channel you have to pay for."

"You recruiting me? You sound like one of the assistants."

"Like I said, man. I don't know jack about college or football or California. I'm stuck here building engines for Mike's Speed Shop, and racing when the entry fee is cheap. You get all the girls. Coaches all over the country beg you to come to their school. Watching you, I wish I'd started football when we were in middle school. C'mon, man. If anything, I'm jealous." Gunner stared out over the surf, eyes wide and thinking.

Just then, one of the rods began to buzz. Toby jumped to it. The buzz turned into screaming.

Gunner was slow to move. Drowsy from the beer he asked, "You got him, Toby?"

"Think so," Toby said, his heart lifting. This is what they'd come for. He dug his heels into the sand and started pulling. Gunner watched for the first hour but then dozed off, leaving Toby to bring in the catch himself.

It turned out to be a two-hour fight. Victorious at last, Toby skinned out the sides and the jaws and tossed them in the cooler. With little help from the rising star, he loaded the gear and put Gunner to bed in the passenger seat.

On the way back to town, he slipped quietly under the gas station light. Melanie was locking the front door of the store, slumped but still irresistible to a local boy. His eyes twinkled as he thought about his own future. He coasted up next to her in his truck, rolled down the window, and put his finger to his lips. He whispered, "Don't wake up the dread pirate Dozy Boozy." Gunner was passed out with his head laying on the dropped window.

She giggled and said, "I told you not to come by with those smelly sharks, Toby." She pushed her hair out of her eyes and placed her hands on her hips.

"I couldn't wait to talk to you. Gunner is leaving town on the next plane out. What say me and you go shark fishing one night?

"Well, Mr. Toby Beaumont Durante," she said formally,

as only a southern girl can. It was loud enough for Gunner to reposition his slouch.

He grinned and cautioned, "Shhhh."

Melanie lowered her voice. "I thought all you were interested in was fast cars and fishing. You want to take me out? It's gonna cost ya'. I've been waiting my whole life for your dumbass."

He leaned his head out the window. "I can't bear to see a good thing go to waste."

"I'm not going anywhere but home. It's late. Call me tomorrow," she said with a come get me look. "Maybe I'll answer."

Toby smiled. "I hope for my sake you do."

"Try me," she said, tossing her hair. As she walked away to her small car, she turned back to see if Toby was still watching. And he was.

• • •

A year later, home from a honeymoon, they sat together on the couch in Melanie's parent's house. The ULA college football game was on. Toby's parents sipped drinks on the porch. During half-time, Gunner's Hollywood smile, under a guacamole green hat, flashed across the screen. He chortled his scripted line. "Try Rockin' Avocado's. The best vegan burger in California. And the best avocado toast on the west coast..."

It took a minute for the laughter in the house to die down. Melanie's momma hollered from the kitchen where she was frying shark nuggets, "We best have some grandbabies by next summer. I get lonely around here."

Toby's mom affirmed the notion from the porch, "Ain't that the truth!"

Toby's dad looked at Melanie's father and asked, "Gus, you want to shoot some targets before the third quarter?"

"I'll have to borrow Melanie's pistol. I don't know how to shoot."

Toby turned his eyes up to the ceiling feigning repentance.

GOOD FRIDAY

'T was Good Friday, and the end of my week-long penance. By the Grace of God, I was out on parole and sitting in a ring of chairs in the basement of St. Pete's Cathedral surrounded by other combatants of the legal system. Tuned for the jealousy of others, my ears picked up rumors, accusations and leaky indictments. My court-appointed, self-help counselor raised his bushy eyebrows and asked me, "Do you remember being fished out of the bay and handcuffed on the deck of a Coast Guard cutter, Boozer?" He wore a pastoral robe and I could see his clenched fists underneath. "Caught on camera diving off the bridge? You made the news."

"I don't own a TV," I replied, still a bit unsteady from the week's abstinence, but happy to be free.

The meeting ended, and I got up from my chair and walked to the folding table, where I dropped my attendance sheet in front of the padre. He signed it, and reminded me with a look, "See you tomorrow."

"Maybe. I like to spread myself around," I replied with a superior wink. I folded the paper and tucked it in the front pocket of my green plaid jacket.

"If you're not here tomorrow, I'll let the Chief know

you've taken your rehabilitation off site. I'm sure he'll be thrilled."

"Whatever," I mumbled, walking out the door with my palm-sized cup of coffee. Finally, I was relieved of my morning commitment, a spiritual advisor imparting wisdom to the inquiring drunk.

My sage advice, on the other hand, should be avoided at all costs—but I couldn't be bothered to explain the nuances of genius. I had been a guest of the Chief's the last six days and was anxious to begin checking the boxes on a long to-do list.

Strolling down the sidewalk, I smelled fried bread wafting in the breeze, my mouth watering with every whiff. The clouds parted and spring resurrected life on the wharf, what may have been missed by the glorious expectation of the Rising Son.

Community service, insisted upon by my false accusers, was the tug of incarceration's sticky grip. For this duty I had to choose wisely. My back might get pitched in for the garden club or the recycling center. But I was a resourceful man locked in an unfair system. Thus, I intended to serve the community five blocks over at Joe's Fish Market and Beignets.

My alligator-skinned loafers had a large gap between my toes and the end of the shoes. It was a mild inconvenience I endured for style. I turned my knee forward, whipped the heel on the upswing and shoved my toes into the landing. Each shoe clicked with the original owner's heel- and toe-taps, in all their reptilian glory. They made a tap-tap clacking on the concrete as I walked, and I threw in an occasional skip or a half-step combo. The tartan couture draped over my shoulders like a rain jacket slung over a metal chair. Fortunately for my thin skin, my jacket sleeves came to my knuckles. The extra fabric absorbed the spilling coffee's heat. I pulled out a cigarette, tossed in my mouth and lit it, then pulled a long draw and snapped my fingers.

I shifted the cup to my left hand to sling my right hand free of hot coffee, but ended up completely dousing my hand to the ends of my fingers. Wincing in pain from the sting, my eyes narrowed and watered. The fog of cigarette smoke formed a could around my head. I imagined an audience for the ridiculous scene and heard children laughing.

The sound came from a yellow bus, parked in the lot between me and the short walk to Joe's beignet stand. A small blonde-haired girl leaned out the front window and said, "You sure do have funny hair, Mister."

"Why, thank you," I said, caught off guard by the compliment. I ran my fingers through my salt-and-pepper locks, thrilled with the bit of attention. My hair had a smell of saltwater, which inexplicably lingered from that one fabulous night, six dry days ago. My fingers snagged in a tangle.

The girl had her fingers folded together supporting her chin on the half-dropped bus window. She said, "You can put napkins in the ends of your shoes to keep 'em from slingin'." My mouth dropped, as she giggled at my epiphany.

Shifting my gaze away from her, I saw a brown-haired boy with a crew cut contort himself through the back window of the bus. First, his arm twisted out, followed by his whole head. He folded his fist under his armpit while pumping out fart sounds and yelled, "Hey, Boozer! Will you tap dance for a dollar? I'll pay you tomorrow."

The boy's noise and joke ignited peals of laughter from the other children on board. I thought about the phantom dollar, but knew from a lifetime of deals to-good-to-be-true, this offer was likely, too, a scam. Shaking my head, I gracefully declined. In a burst of cigarette smoke, I tap-tapped across the parking lot to the beignet stand, my quick retreat causing one of my heel-taps to fly off into the gutter with a clang. Now, with one leg extended in a half kick, I glided on the other heel tap and crashed into the ordering booth.

"One lemon beignet, please," I said, steadying myself on the bar. I threw my coffee cup in the trash, then stubbed out what was left of my cigarette short and dropped it in my pocket for later. The register rang as I paid with a five-dollar-bill. Now, I only had the twenty the Chief tipped me for waxing his police car. I saved it for a purchase in Joe's.

Assuming what some Eastern religions describe as Zen pose, I sat down, hypnotized by the steam rising from the dusted white perfection of the beignet. Powdered sugar on top superheated into globules. Pastor Bill of the First Baptist Church sat down next to me. He was an overly large man with a handsome face. His suit had the rough, off-white look of circus-tent material. It was capped off by a pastel bowtie in the shape of two Easter eggs connected at the small ends by a marble. I hadn't seen him in ages. Wrapping his cavernous jaw around his chocolate-Easter-bunny beignet, he asked between chews, "Boozer, do you know Jesus?"

I searched for the right words. "I'm grateful to my mother that introduced us. I'm not so grateful to a municipal court system that reminds me monthly I'm not Him." I innocently rested my chin on my clasped fingers, using the green plaid jacket sleeve as a pillow.

He stopped chewing. His smile pinched his eyes together. "Train up a child in the way he should go. That's Bible, Boozer. Your momma taught you right!"

"My last decade has far out-punted her best expectations," I smirked. "I think she wanted me to be a lawyer. She'd be proud, though. I've spent enough time in the public defender's office to pass the Bar." In my hand the pastry had cooled with the conversation, and I took my first bite. It was lemony ecstasy. I could almost hear harps ringing in my ears. "Preacher, you think there'll be lemon beignets in heaven?"

"I'm betting on it. I'll ask Joe to deliver these chocolate ones," Pastor Bill replied, holding up his pastry as a sermon illustration. He twisted his head to face me. "Glad I'm not Catholic. There's no way I could go without these for Lent."

"I heard that! Why do you think we have the whole beignet stand to ourselves?"

"Say, you got' real questions about heaven?" Pastor Bill pressed, not yet letting go of the spiritual interrogation he'd started.

"Nah. Most days, I pray to see God's will... Since I've got your undivided attention, though, I do have a question." I sucked out the lemon center of my beignet.

His hands dropped to the table, his beignet resting in

them as he focused on me. "What is it, Boozer? Jesus knows every hair on your head and has loved you for eternity. God's love burns bright."

"Ok. If Main Street Baptist on Main is the oldest church around, why is your church named the First Baptist Church?"

Spiritually disappointed, he re-engaged his beignet and finished it in one bite. He tossed his wrapper in the trash, and said offhandedly, "Your granddaddy Boozer picked Main Street Baptist. We took what was left." He stood to depart.

"Main Street Baptist was founded on a long line of Boozers, Preacher. Sounds like the Baptist have an unbeatable expansion strategy," I said to the back of his head.

"It's called the Great Commission, Professor Boozer," he said, walking off. Then he paused and turned, "Y' know? You could be cleaning church pews instead of washing police cars for community service," as if he and the Chief traded inside knowledge to benefit from cheap labor.

"Did Jesus tell you I've been washing police cars?" Startled by his spot-on intuition, I chuckled and then probed the opportunity. "Maybe I could serve a few hours under the roof at your church." Sensing he wanted a firm reply, I added, "I'll pray on it," giving Pastor Bill the non-commitment of a strong maybe.

He clicked his cheek in warning. "God's love burns hot, too, Boozer. My offer won't last long," he said, and left.

The doughy Lord's Supper of fried bread and lemon partaken, I brushed the signs of sugary addiction from my hands with a handful of napkins. Then I bent down and jammed them in the ends of the gators and re-inserted my feet. With a smoother stride from a snug fit, I three-tapped to the end of the processional topped with yarmulkes and faded baseball caps next door. The line was following one after the other into Joe's. I snapped-turned to join the end as an ROTC cadet might join a formation. Another heel-tap flew off.

Joe's Fish Market vibrated with social interaction and ringing cash registers. Ice water tubs brimmed with enough shrimp to floor-sweep the Gulf of Mexico from Cape San Blas to Bayou La Batre. The owner, Joe, sat just inside on his grandfather's barstool. It was built from Greek whaling harpoons, as the story goes, and was stationed next to the open hallway separating the ice-house from the market. Joe could see the boat docks, the fish cleaners and the entire market from his seat. Over his shoulder, a yellowfin tuna was being truncated and carved on a smooth, stainless-steel altar. Next to the duck-billed hat covering Joe's bald head was a loudspeaker mouthpiece that hung from the ceiling. Standing at the rear of the assembled masses, I tried to pose as an interested bystander and not look like a prisoner-one-day-removed. I leaned over to the Turn-O-Matic and pulled number 16.

And there she was. Jesse's shoulder blades rested on the wall freezers while her rump pressed the glass. She stood tall atop her cork wedge shoes. Suspended from her naked arm, the thin strap of her bag dangled from the crease in her elbow. When our eyes met, she shifted in her dress and raised her free hand to caress the top of her hip until her fingers floated to a stop.

"You're a toe-tappin, rattlin rogue, aren't you, Boozer?" she teased.

I smiled and snapped my fingers. "You like my shoes, Jesse?"

"I sure do. I bought them for my uncle."

"I bought these at the thrift-store. Are you suggesting...?"

"My uncle's dead, Boozer," she interrupted, "But, yeah, I like 'em. I bought 'em, didn't I?" She crossed her arms, cradling her long red fingernails in her elbows and turned to face me. Her lips creased as she looked me up and down, from my tangled hair down to my shiny gators, and pronounced her judgment. "You look good."

I tugged my belt up, showcasing the entire length of the gators. "What do you like most about them?"

Her eyes gauged me below the bangs of her curly black wig. Lifting her investigative fingernail to her cheek, she said, "I don't know yet."

Around her the fish market was a beehive of activity. Porters pushed shovels, the white plastic edges scraping under the rock hides of oysters piled on the ice-house floor. A porter behind us emptied buckets of ice into a tub-cooler shaped like a rolling laundry basket. Joe shoved his white rubber boot in the bottom rung of his stool. Raising the receiver to his inverted ship's bow of a nose, his voice squawked like a benevolent God—if God was a pelican. "Number 13! Royal Reds seven-ninety-nine-a pound. All you 'ave to do is ask." His h's dropped as a matter of convenience, or as I suspected, an homage to Melville's Captain Ahab.

Rabbi Sol, a head taller than the assembled crowd and capped in a yarmulke, raised the winning ticket in his hand. His dark-haired wife Gloria held his other hand, her face shaped in centuries of carefully selected Jewry and large round sunglasses.

"Nice to see you again, Rabbi," Joe's voice crackled through the loudspeaker. It had the intended effect. Rabbi Sol caught Joe's eye and his curiosity grew from just looking to buying.

"What'll it be," an attendant with pigtails wrapped in a red-rubber-apron squealed.

Approaching the glass, Sol cupped his hand over his mouth and hollered, "How much is the triggerfish, Joe?"

Joe squawked from several feet away, "Eight-ninety-nine-a-pound for the triggerfish, plus Caesar's share. 'Is taxes must be paid."

Sol responded, "That seems high."

Joe grinned. "Add a dollar. We've cobia, redfish, and flounder for the same."

"What?!" Sol exclaimed, bucking the increased price.

"The rainy days and broken steerage weren't priced in my first offer," Joe said. As he spoke, a pair of ice tongs slipped out of a deck hand's grip. They clattered and clanged across the floor, shot off the edge of the concrete, ricocheted off a boat hull, and dropped into the water with a splash. Joe bowed his head and pinched the bow of his nose.

"Three pounds of triggerfish, please," Sol said to Pigtails, not wanting to see prices go any higher.

My gaze was riveted to Jesse's side profile. Out of the corner of my eye, I watched Sol's wife walk to the wine shop. My eyes then wandered back to the curve of Jesse's hour glass shape.

"Number 14. Snapper and Grouper. Ten-ninety-nine-a pound," the loudspeaker squawked. The electric voice jolted the room.

"Like what you see?" Jesse pursed her lips and almost invited. Her wig twirled on her neck and caught my eyes before I'd raised them to hers.

"Who wouldn't," I said, my filter dulled from a week in lock-up.

Pastor Bill made his way into the market. His ham-fisted hand shot up. "Number 14! That'll be me, Joe. Send me to the catfish. Plenty of mouths to feed." His arm waved his ticket like he was the next guy in line for salvation.

Joe busied himself with Pastor Bill's request as Pig Tails, who was chewing gum, called out to Sol, "Triggerfish skinned or unskinned?" Her gloved fingers drooped above the reshuffled fish slabs. She leveled her eyes at Sol, blew a bubble and popped it with her tongue, and blurted, "The skin is thick."

"...to protect against the underworld's persecution," I joked to Jesse.

"Skinned," Sol responded with the prudence of a Pharisee, his arms crossed.

I felt her lips move against my ear as she stoked the furnace. "Never-ending persecution." Shaking, I fought to keep my eyes open when she slithered around my arm.

The glint of Pig Tail's blade flashed until the fish were hollowed. Two skin flaps attached to the same spine hung from her knife. She cast the rubbish of sinew aloft, their souls exiled to a carcass barrel, and their flesh flipped into the scales. Quickly priced and tagged, she half-tossed the twist-tied bag over the glass. It hung between her finger-tips. "Three pounds," she said. "Any Royal Reds, Sol? They just came in."

"No shrimp for me, thanks!" Sol recoiled, nearly dropping the bag when Pig Tails released it. He recovered it with both hands and came toward us.

"P'shaw!" Jesse hollered to Pig Tails, "I'll take what he don' want, soon as Captain Joe calls my number." She bucked her wig with a nod and turned her attention back to the Rabbi. "What's wrong with you, Sol? You don't eat shrimp?"

"No," he smiled. His pointed mouth grinned into the cleft dividing the neckline of her spandex. "The Torah's been my guiding light thus far. I'm sure to finish my days breathing in its glow." He reviewed us both with a quick look.

"I'm finishing my day with shrimp gumbo, Lord willin'." Jesse clutched my hand as she spoke to Sol. My heart pulsed when she pecked me on the cheek. "Where's Gloria?" she asked. Jesse turned back to me and raised one of her eyebrows.

"I think I saw her walking into the wine shop," I explained. As Sol turned to leave, I asked, "Before you go, is there any need of my skills at your synagogue? I'm in another dustup with the Chief."

"Hmm," he thought, raising his hand to his beard. "Can you retell of the Exodus in Yiddish?"

"My Yiddish is a little rusty," I sighed. "Hey, don't you sponsor a film festival? A gentleman in the parking lot offered me a dollar to tap dance."

"Perhaps you have a creative idea, Boozer. We could use a fresh act for the film festival. Maybe a vaudeville theme. And we always need ushers."

"Sol, I was thinking I could star in the first act or possibly a choreography," I offered, bemused.

"Maybe you should've taken the offer in the parking lot." His brows furrowed as he ended the conversation. "I must be getting to Gloria," he said with a growing panic to leave.

"Boozer, you're so cute. When were you going to tell me about this? Maybe I can cook for you," Jesse redirected my attention. Between two fingernails, she held a twenty-dollar bill before me.

Delirious from her perfume and not comprehending when she'd lifted my car washing money, I stammered, "Can, uh, we cook at your place? My roommates wouldn't understand."

"Of course, baby," she committed.

Next to the row of cash registers, Pastor Bill consoled a somber but radiantly attractive widow. He jockeyed for position in front of another young admirer in a baseball cap, already on the job. Joe slid Pastor Bill's cooler back across the concrete, the scratch of plastic signaling Bill's order completed. Bill stopped it with his foot and bid the widower adieu. Bill called back to Joe, in affront to the trinity of local religions, "Thanks. Can I get a volume discount? Protestants don't have a nation-state like Rome or Israel."

"Nor the overhead," Joe retorted, followed with a Bible dart. "Tell them at the exchange to cut your bill ten percent. You can 'ave the Lord's share I was going to give 'im.

Number 15! Who's number 15?"

A small habit with a nun inside stepped to the counter. With the voice of an angry song bird lilting with an Irish accent, she defended free will and the tolerance of all. "Well, that's a fine how-do-you-do," she said to Pastor Bill's wagging finger as he walked away. "The Baptists have an unmatched majority on the earth upon which we stand, but Pastor Bill must go draggin' the good name of the Pope and God's Chosen into a fish market, and on our mutual day of mourning our Lord and Savior." She calmed herself, while clutching a ticket in her upturned hands like a sacrament before Joe.

"What'll it be, Sister Mary Catherine McGuire?" he asked, his first time not using the loudspeaker.

"I pity the poor paddy, Joe," Sister McGuire said, no stranger to bargaining as the sole heiress to North Florida's largest seafood restaurant franchise.

"For Pete's sake, Sister," Joe said, shaking his head, "tell me what 'ast befallen your poor paddies that I may pity them, too."

"These snapper prices they're taking home to their mother. She's sure to punish the poor paddy for adding beignets. What'll I tell my own orphans, whose insolence only grows bolder after a week of mullet?"

"Tell them the wages of life pays the bills, and the wages of sin is death."

"But the orphan knows of no costs, nor the wisdom of your years, Joe. Only the certainty of their empty stomach."

He sighed, helpless before her persuasions. "Tell them the price 'as been paid by the 'eavenly Father. It's snapper and key lime pies for Easter, Sister Mary Catherine. And tell your father 'e's getting the best fish prices on the Gulf Coast." His bent elbow snapped the receiver back under the hook of his nose as he commanded, "Meet Sister Mc-Guire around back and fill 'er order." And without another mention of charity, "Number 16! Number 16! Sacrament in the Wine Shop. Red, White, and Beer."

Momentarily inebriated from Joe's invitation, I kept the main thing the main thing. I reached for a golden ring, the cradle of charity. "Peace be with you, Sister."

"Well, hello, Mr. Boozer. I didn't see you standing there." Mary Catherine's green eyes, emotionless under the habit, raked back and forth between Jesse and me. Her eyes came about. "Hello, Jesse."

Jesse looked at me, frowned, and told me more than asked me, "Aren't we Number 16, baby?"

"Uh, yes, we are," I said, looking down at the ticket in my hand.

Jesse snatched the ticket from my hand and walked toward Pig Tails. I heard her over Sister McGuire's shoulder. "Pound and a half of Royal Reds. Biggest you got." Jesse turned her gaze back to us, her wig slipping on her scalp under her rotating neck, the smirk of judgement on her lips.

"Sister McGuire," I said, praying to her God she wouldn't see Jesse's show, "are you in need of any help at your church? Maybe I could help in the church choir?"

"Oh, Mr. Boozer, how kind of you," she said, "but I'm in such a rush." As she turned, she stopped. With a look of possibility, she said, "We do need a bus driver."

"That'd be perfect, had the Chief not taken my driver's license."

"That's a shame, Mr. Boozer, but thanks for the offer." She walked past Joe to the ice house, and the pointillist hue of her freckled face faded under her habit. So close I was!

Jesse came back over, her perfume leading the way, with a twisted bag of shrimp the size of railroad spikes. We proceeded to the line of cash registers. Jesse's wig readjusted and her arm coiled around my green plaid as she handed me the bag. But then, abruptly, she turned and walked away. "Where're you going?" I asked her.

The shine from the back of her legs stopped shimmering when she turned back. "Don't worry, baby. I'm just going to get us a bottle of wine." Her red mini-dress twisted in the middle, crushing the flower imprinted at her waistline. "Red or White?"

"Get whatever you like under—" I said, resigned to irrelevance as the wine shop door closed behind her "—ten dollars."

After an eternity in line, the attendant said, "Next." I handed her the bag of shrimp. She scanned it and asked, "Is that it?"

Looking over to the wine shop door and said, "No, my lady's coming with a bottle of wine." A porter dumped another load of ice in a tub-cooler and cut his eyes at me sideways.

"Well, your lady better hurry up or meet you at the back of the line."

"Ok. I'll hurry. What's the damage from the shrimp?"

"Eleven-sixteen," she demanded.

I handed her the twenty and looked back just in time to

see Gloria, Sol, and Jesse spilling out of the wine shop. The attendant put the change on the counter and said, "Next!"

Jesse toasted their plastic wine glasses, jiggled over to me, and said to no one in particular, "...and this, too." Carrying it by the neck, she set the bottle next to the change.

The attendant shook her head, rolled her eyes, and grabbed the bottle. "Nine dollars. It's on sale." The porter snickered to himself as he dumped more ice into the tub.

I grimaced, eyed the bursting dam of her neckline again, and dug into my jacket pockets. "I need sixteen cents," I asked Jesse out loud—and God silently.

Jesse leaned into my ear again, "Almost home." She plumbed the depths of my green plaid pocket with her hand running over mine. "Jackpot," she purred, fishing out a quarter. She tossed it on the counter and said, "Keep the change." She yanked the bag of shrimp and grabbed the wine bottle by the neck. We walked out together.

Behind us, I heard the porter laugh and the cashier holler, "Next!" Under me, my last two taps tapped under my gators. Standing on the sidewalk I said, hopefully, "Bon Appetit? To your place?"

From a parked position in the far corner of the parking lot, a rusty hotrod with T-tops rumbled itself into a smoking tempest. Sputtering and coughing, it roared up, moved closer and screeched to a halt in front of us. The driver wore a black motorcycle helmet without a face shield, the exposed steel snaps framing his milky white mug. His eyes wandered as if connected to two different brains, meandering like search lights in the fog. He revved the engine.

Deaf from the mechanical roar, I buckled in fear. Before I could lean in to protect her, Jesse reached for the door handle, swung it open, and hopped in with our dinner. Confused and bewildered, I watched as she slammed the door, cracked the cap on the wine bottle, and tipped it straight up through her open tee-top.

The hotrodder's face contorted under his black helmet and his eyes floated into focus, like the answer in the plastic window of a magic 8-ball. He flared his lips and nostrils, revealing at least one missing tooth.

In a last breath of hope, I flubbed the delivery. "Are you coming back, Jesse?"

Through the faraway mist of bloodshot eyes, the magic 8-Ball blurted out, "Don't count on it!" Blood pumped through a vessel rooted in his forehead. A vein streaked down his neck and under the shoulder strap of his white tank top. His middle finger, sheathed in a silver skull ring, burst upward in front of the canyon of Jesse's cleavage. His eyes then wandered through his windshield to his future, as he taunted, "Thanks for dinner shrimp dick!" Then, he jerked the gear shifter down, over, and up.

I stumbled back and exhaled. "Jesse? What about..."

He stomped on the gas, and all hell broke loose. The engine revved as the hotrod's tires whined and boiled. The back end of the car slowly drifted on the screaming rubber, where it met the road. The hotrodder's driver-side-eye was fixed on the way forward while his passenger-side-eye remained, momentarily, on me. Circling, they recalculated, and I prayed he'd take the path away from the yellow school bus.

The brown-haired boy with the crew cut had come up to the driver's seat of the bus in an act of parking-lot boredom. Through the bus door's glass, I could see both his and the little blond-haired girl's eyes, round as their opened mouths. He began to yank the brake handle back-and-forth. I heard a pop. Suddenly, the bus jolted and began to slowly roll backward.

The bus creeped in reverse as the fishtailing hotrod hurtled forward. The black arc of tire marks on the pavement pointed directly at the bus. The connection sounded when the hotrod's back tail light exploded on the bus's front bumper, eliciting a scream from the children. Still rolling backwards, the bus's back bumper came to rest against a parking lot guard rail.

The duo shot out onto Main Street like a rudderless ship, exposed wires and broken tail lights flailing and banging off the back. Two middle fingers thrust through both sides of the T-top. One bright red fingernail shot off the neck of an open wine bottle and the other, a silver skull-ring pushed high by a foundation of pig knuckles.

With the angry courage of every victim in the rear-view mirror, the brown-haired boy shook his fist from his driver's seat window.

I was startled when Sister Mary Catherine McGuire behind me whispered, "Glory be."

Still in shock, I turned to see she was leading a porter, who breathed, "Praise Jesus and Sister Mary Catherine's rosary beads."

She came to a halt next to me, dropping her rosaries in a secret pocket. The porter rested his arm on the dolly stacked with frozen boxes. "Mr. Boozer, do you know the driver of that car?" Sister Mary Catherine asked. The porter chuckled.

"No. Why would you think that?"

"You two share so much in common," she said, as she motioned for the porter to follow her. After the porter loaded Easter lunch onto the bus, she turned her head in the dissipating smoke and said in her best Lenten Irish, "Happy Easter, Mr. Boozer. Peace be with you."

With the fresh optimism of introspection, I replied, "You, too, Sister Mary Catherine McGuire." I pulled the last two toe-taps from my gators, finally comfortable in the green skin.

Sitting in the driver's seat doing the community service she'd offered me, Sister McGuire cranked the bus and bounced out of the parking lot. The voices of laughing children echoed from the dropped windows.

I pulled the short from my pocket and relit it. I inhaled the last of the smoldering nicotine, blew out the smoke and flicked the filter in the drain grate. I swung my head around to the parking lot. There to my lonely eyes did appear Pastor Bill, leaning against his long four-door sedan and eating another chocolate bunny beignet. I walked over with great humility. In his backseat, I noticed a brown paper bag, shaped like a six-pack, atop his cooler of catfish. I pointed to the six-pack and asked, "From a strictly doctrinal point of interest, did you get everything you need?"

He took a bite of his second chocolate-bunny-beignet and said through the melting dough, "Beer-battered catfish don't batter themselves. If I drink a couple, that's between me and Jesus." He shook his head and said before taking another bite, "What about your smoking problem? You's choking on it over there in the parking lot."

I confessed without recognition of the entire event, "Yeah, I should quit."

Pastor Bill swallowed. "Did you get everything you need, Boozer?"

"Depends. Do you still have an opening cleaning church pews?"

"Dusting church pews instead of police cars was a good deal an hour ago."

I ran my fingers through the tangle of hair and melted tire rubber. "What do you mean by was?"

He swallowed another bite, clicked his cheek, and said, "The fella' you saw me talking to, here with his mother, got the job."

"His mother, huh?! What else you got?"

"Toilets," he said and brushed the sugar off his hands by slapping them together. "You'll be closer to the Throne of God since the day you gave up the sauce."

Regret gripped my stomach. Desperation mixed with the memory of my last drink overwhelmed me. "Oh, well. Toilets are smaller than police cars," I said, grateful for the air conditioning at my new job.

"Good! We get a big crowd on Easter," he said. "We'll see if cleaning crappers can keep you out of the frying pan.

RESCUES

Our fishing experiences on our first dates were corner-
stones of our marriage, or so I thought. For me, these
had become cherished memories. Paige's recollections go
in a different direction, ranging from moments of isolated
terror to unhinged boredom, waterlogged with sea sickness. She deserved a medal, a big one, strung from diamonds. When I mentioned it, she suggested hand-mined
diamonds—my hands.

Paige's line-and-pole saga began on a trip to my home
fishing grounds in North Florida. I insisted on an August
trip during our first beach vacation together. It was a less-
than-ideal time for fishing in the region, as fish don't bite
when it's hotter than seven hells.

Her final fishing adventure was not long after. It unfolded in picturesque Playa Flamingo, Costa Rica; the land
of Pura Vida. One mile out past the cove's safety, the serene
waters swelled to rollers, tossing the boat. The captain set
the bait on outriggers as we trolled through the water, bobbing and twisting through liquid humps shaped like mo-
guls on a ski slope. With each wave, the outriggers, once
level with the tower, dipped to touch the water's surface.

Paige lay prostrate on the boat floor seasick. She dis-
played both remarkable courage and misplaced trust in

my weather forecast. I was mesmerized by the schools of blue fin tuna leaping from the water, desperate to escape the billfish skyrocketing from the deep to feed. Her whimpers of pain, though, cast a pall over the excursion. Just as she managed to crawl onto a gear locker, my deep bait line tightened. Reeling in the largest roosterfish ever witnessed by any of the crew on board didn't cure Paige's nausea. My triumph made it worse. Nevertheless, with the self-sacrifice worthy of a two-year-old, I asked her to snap a picture.

Paige never did anything halfway. Her commitment to our new marriage was tantamount to a kamikaze pilot. My wife-warrior pulled the camera from her purse and snapped the last shot on the cheap camera. Just then, another roller knocked it from her hands. She lunged to the side of the boat and threw up into the water as the camera slid under a boat bench. I considered framing the picture of mine and the deckhand's feet, but thought better of memorializing the moment. It was our last time out on a boat together.

Paige was no stranger to loss and heartbreak. Our wandering paths crossed and we came together. As we went along, our joy multiplied and our misery halved. She could recognize the need for a change and occasionally made one that added to our relationship.

Paige spearheaded my journey into the world of rescue dogs. She'd had a number of them in her life. One evening on the couch, she broached the subject with quiet resolve. "Burr, we're getting a dog. Are you okay with rescues?" Without waiting for my unwanted answer, she concluded, "Good." I immediately resigned to the fact that the deal was already done. I dropped the market reports in my lap and looked over my glasses. "Sure, babe. I love all dogs; big ones, little ones, barky ones, quiet ones, but I especially love rescue bull dogs," I replied in support of where I heard her going.

The following Sunday morning, we met Chloe: sweet, precious Chloe. The fawn and white on her nose spread over her sleepy green eyes. She drifted off like a four-legged baby in my maw-and-paw-in-law's sunroom chair, which she had immediately claimed as her own. Any apprehension of her square jaws melted away with her childlike snore. She had a little block head and a kiss for everyone.

From Chloe's first day, every day after was better—until her last. The pride of the morning walk and the belle of the backyard for ten years, Chloe's presence brought immeasurable happiness. Then came her heartbreaking diagnosis of Addison's disease. That concluded in one of the worst days of our shared life. We prayed, and let her go.

For months afterward, we continued through life with a dog sized hole in the house. In the void left by her absence, I sought solace by visiting rescue centers. I would text pictures of new pups to Paige. It gave me a sense of purpose, being ready to renew the puppy-job that had filled our home for those years. Paige, ever empathetic, held off until the time was right. She cautioned after more pictures, "I'll tell you when I'm ready."

"Yes, dear. Love you—mean it. I'll be home in a minute." I paused awaiting her reply, and then lost patience. "Say it back."

"Say what back?"

"That you love me."

"I love you."

The patience required for finding just the right pure-bred specimen didn't fit our emotional need for immediate satisfaction. For any that wondered if we had apprehension about a mixed breed, they only needed to count the turn-around time from adoption kennel to the permanent dog bowl next to our kitchen sink. The dollars saved buying a drive-through dog went straight to the dog bone budget. Their block heads were a priceless bonus.

During the following Christmas, we laid on the couch watching our favorite story. Paige taped her daytime stories, and we'd watch them at night. That's what Paige called them—"stories." It might seem an odd choice for TV entertainment, but that Victor, he's a hustler. She said she would tell me when she was ready. A few weeks later and it was just like that—she turned off the TV and looked at me. "We're getting another dog."

The words lay over me like Chloe's blanket we kept on the couch. We needed a change. Paige pulled her phone and showed me the picture. There on the rescue dog app was Jaws, wrapped in a Santa Claus beard, his green eyes matching Chloe's, but his lonely and bloodshot. "How can you be so sure? I've shown you dozens of pictures of rescues."

"This is the one. His name is Jaws and we're picking him up Thursday afternoon. Can you get off work?"

"Sure. I guess. If you're sure," I said. To cement the deal, I asked again. "You're sure?"

"I'm sure. I already called the rescue center. All we have do is be there Friday."

"I'm ready if you're ready." We hugged it out and got excited.

Friday morning came with a shock neither of us needed. Paige texted me at work, "They gave Jaws away." When my phone rang, I could hear her on the other end crying, "Why did they do that? I feel like I've lost Chloe all over again."

"Oh, babe. I'm so sorry," I said, engrossed in work. A couple of months prior, the stock market began a real swoon. Not one of those little dips, a bear market. Ringing phones begat emotionally frayed clients. Who could blame them? The market dove even deeper in front of me on the computer screen. "We'll get another one," I mumbled about the rescue dog, trailing off with the downward sloping charts. It was the best I could manage in a day that was filled with talk of losses.

"Another one? We're getting Jaws," she bellowed and blew her nose. "I left them my phone number for when they bring him back," she sniffled. "Pray with me."

"Ok, babe." I was still fumbling for words from her news about Jaws, mixed with the news that the stock market was canceling Christmas. "What are we praying for?"

"That they'll bring him back to the rescue center." She began in the earnest way of any prayer of intercession. "Dear God, I don't ever ask for anything important, but this is important. Thank you for Jaws, and please don't punish me because my husband is a fool. Please bring Jaws back to the rescue center so we can have him and he can save Christmas. Amen."

"Amen. Love you, babe. The phone's ringing off the hook. Gotta go."

"Me, too. Love you."

Paige was taking it hard, and the rescue center's administrative slip up, even if out of our control, didn't help. Trying to ring in some yuletide cheer, we went shopping for some family gifts. I took an opening as we loaded bags of presents into the car, and tried to explain to her that God always answers prayers. It's just that sometimes the answer is "no," because He has better things in store.

"You're so annoying," she replied. Like an alarm bell, her phone rang. She answered, "Yes." Pause. "Yes." She looked straight ahead into the parking lot, listened and said, "Yes. We'll be there in 45 minutes. Please don't give our dog away again!" She hung up the phone and said, "Drive. They brought Jaws back. He's coming home. Wait, stop!"—a quick bow of her head and—"Please God, don't let them give our dog away again. Ok, now go! Go!"

I raced out of the parking lot and launched onto the road, weaving in and out of lanes. Paige pushed me faster, then slower, then faster. "Speed up! Yellow is partly green. Don't you see those brake lights? Speed up!" It was like driving anywhere else with her, except on this trip I appreciated the helpful navigation. Our boy was close.

About fifteen minutes later we parked at the animal shelter and got out. I tried to reassure her. "Babe. This is going to be a process."

"Whatever. See you inside," she tossed back and bolted to the door.

I caught up to her as a male attendant began escorting Paige to the holding area in the back. The room echoed with howling and barking rescues begging for a chance at a home.

The attendant offered us ear plugs, left for a moment, then came back. He pushed open the holding area door with his back and whirled around with a six-month-old puppy-muscle squirming in hands. His nose was longer than his body and his head sat on top, eyes taking in every possible thing he could see. He wiggled loose from the attendant's hands and did a quick four-point landing as his biscuit paws hit the floor. He raced around us as we stood in the small lobby area, if for nothing more than to burn off the steam inherent in the breed. Thankfully, his ears were still intact, flopping on the sides of his head like dish rags as he circled the room full speed. His little back nails skidded to the outside like a drift-car, his back half out of sync with his front as he chased the excitement of the moment. His full-length tail was stiff as a pencil. After his fourth time around, ignoring all of us in the room, I stuck my arm out. He crashed into it and began to lick us both.

Paige grabbed him from me and said, "You've had enough." Drawing the puppy close into her arms, she said, "You're safe now, baby boy," as he squirmed and licked.

The attendant chuckled. "He saved himself, that one. We had to chase him through three neighborhoods before he came to the treats."

She came up from her nose muzzle on the back of his noggin, stroking a bump on his side. "What's this," she asked him, as she rubbed. There in plain sight, like God was trying to yank one of his ribs for a female and he wouldn't let go, the last rib in the row pushed his skin out.

I immediately covered his ears and said, "Don't talk like that in front of him. It'll make him self-conscious, and that could reflect poorly on his grades long-term."

His uncontrollable wiggling made us all laugh. I thought to myself, Good. Maybe he can pick up our morning 5K where Chloe left off.

On the rescue center's temporary rope leash, Jaws had calmed from his initial burst of love, and now trotted in front of Paige with his bulging head and gator jaws held high. I walked behind mentally measuring my office cabinet for a Best-In-Mix Trophy. Paige handed me the leash as we approached the front desk and said, "Hold him." She hefted her purse on the desk and pulled out her checkbook. "Who do I pay?"

The worn-out attendant shrugged and said, "No one. The couple that returned him this morning have already paid for everything."

I crouched next to Jaws and whispered into his ears, "Even better. You're free."

Paige was offended at the thought of him being returned and asked, "Who would bring this angel back?"

"He's got a raging case of kennel cough, miss."

"Pfft," Paige smirked. She ended the short dialogue with gratitude for his volunteerism, and thankfulness for our Christmas present, as she wrote the shelter a check anyway. She even dropped a couple large bills on the desk for lunch.

In the background, I pulled Jaws close and asked him, "Do you like old John Wayne reruns." He answered with another lick.

Fast forward a week, his kennel cough was quickly cured, and he was at home and well fed. His sleep number was tuned to a comfortable range between 35 and 50, depending on the temperature outside. The only thing keeping him from a brisk 5k every morning was Paige's declaration "he should be allowed to sleep in 'til nine on the weekends". He was forced, but that wasn't my decision to make.

His body grew into his long nose, his floppy ears and his big paws. The rib he wouldn't let go of faded into his barrel of a chest. He got so big, if he had a mane, we would've been arrested for lion taming.

Large and in charge, he learned to fetch—or more accurately, he taught me to throw. When he wasn't rubbing his back hair on the carpet begging for a tummy rub, he slept. He was never out of eyesight, always in the same room as one or both of us. When he was ready to play fetch again, he punched me in the nuts, if I didn't see it coming. We learned together.

Jaws became comfortable with our many friends from around the neighborhood, too. The first time Paige received a call because he got out, she answered, "Are you asking for a ransom?" I heard over the speakerphone, "No. We have him here in our house. He's a very friendly boy. Your phone number on his collar was a great idea."

When Paige thanked them and hung up, she glared at me. "You are a fool. I was just kidding before."

"I'll try to be more careful about closing the gates." At that point, I knew an apology and my disappearance for a couple of days would do us both good. I sent a note to Murph, my black-Irish fishing buddy from Savannah. Murph hung around with Jaws and me a couple of nights, when Paige went with her sisters on girls' trip. Jaws and Murph were acquainted, and they left an impression on each other.

Within a week, I heard back. After a phone call to lay out plans, I went down the stairs. I found Paige lying on the couch with Jaws laying lengthwise between her legs with his head in her lap, covered underneath Chloe's blanket. Suspicious, she asked, "Who was that?"

Play it cool, I told myself. "Murph. He's gathering another group for a second chance at South Andros. We'll be flyfishing for bonefish," I stated more than asked.

Jaws wagged his tail when he heard Murph's name, knocking Chloe's blanket off his back end. Paige asked if I could fly fish. "I can a little, babe. I went down there once before." She looked up at me as I tried to explain. "You and I roll-casted in Michigan for salmon, but fly-fishing the Bahamas is much tougher. No candlelit dinners or dune walks. We'll be totally alone, except for the guides. Murph and I have to practice in a rain storm to get anywhere close to live conditions." I made the getaway sound arduous. Jaws, with his body motionless, wagged his tail.

She looked back down at her magazine and turned the page. "Roll casting? Is that what you call your little fishing trips, Burrell? More like role playing if you ask me," she giggled to herself. "Isn't that right sweet baby boy," she said to the lump of fur under her blanket with the black spotted nose. "But you're not asking me, are you? Just you and Murph, right?" She flipped another page without looking up.

I said humbly, "Just our guides Lonnix and Edwin, and

me and Murph." He wagged his tail again as if to cast his vote in my favor.

Paige lifted the magazine above her head and looked at the black nose and said, "Traitor." Then she brought the magazine back to reading level. "What are Lonnix and Edwin like?"

I laughed out loud. "You ever heard of the Sons of Thunder; James and John? Lonnix and Edwin are the sons of Timber. They're built like coastal pine trees and drive fast skiffs for a living." I caught the twitch in her eye and tried to soften my hyperbole, "But we have life vests. And if we're adrift in skinny water, we'll wade to shore. It's not too deep."

"How long?"

My enthusiasm was deflated a little by the tranquil scene in front of me I was asking to leave. "Five days. Three fishing days and two round trip non-stops from Atlanta to Congo Town. Did I mention, South Andros is the bone-fishing capital of the world? The flats are renowned."

"Now this girl knows how to wear a pair of flats." She held up the magazine for me to see. She wondered, "Can you eat bonefish?"

I shrugged and mumbled a made-up bonefish appetizer. Then I thought better of it, looked into her blue eyes and said, "No, babe. They're too boney."

With her reliable sparkle, she said, "Go ahead. Tell Murph I said you could go." Her hand lifted from the magazine, grabbed a Jaws snack and tossed it above his nose. Enormous white teeth emerged from under the blanket and closed on the snack with a snap. Flitting her fingers toward the door to shoo me away, she said, "You owe me a week in Michigan. Bye, bye. Jaws and I are reading."

"I'll start planning it today. Thanks, babe."

To seal the deal, Jaws bounded off the couch galloping like a horse, did a bucking loop around the rug, then ran over and punched me in the nuts. "Doh," I winced. "Time to go throw the ball?" Paige giggled.

We're a family of rescues.

MONEY FLOWED

It was spending season in Washington, D.C. Budgets were passed and money was moving.

The Speaker of the House crossed Constitution Avenue to meet the Chairman of the Federal Reserve on the opposite sidewalk, both in the finest tailored suits. The Congressman's effort provided the Chairman his legislated sense of independence. Upon arrival, the Speaker of the House dispensed the illusion by planting his toe cap so close to the Chaiman's he could count his eyelashes twitching. "Chairman, I've some bad news and some good news. We're spending more money than we make, but you're good for it. Here are the receipts," he said, demanding payment as he waved the paper in his hand. The exchange was a sinister negotiation. The Speaker cautioned against curtailing his own reckless financial decisions.

The Chairman's eyes moved to see a stack of receipts flailing in the Speaker's hands. His eyes twitching and sweat forming on his forehead, he replied, "Again? My God, man. Can't you read? Seventeenth-century Spain paved their streets with gold because their gold was worthless. The Allied Powers chained the Weimar Republic to so much debt, they lashed out with Hitler. Greece? Mexico? Do I even need to go there?"

Indifferent to his qualms and looking past the obvious mistakes of the past, the Speaker said, "C'mon, Chairman. I'll have the Treasury Secretary crank up that printer and make some more fiat money."

"Don't any of you people ever think about inflation? Ever!?"

"Chairman, that's your department. We all know if you really wanted to stop inflation and climate change, you'd triple interest rates." In an affable demeanor of persuasion, the Speaker let out a compromise. "I mean, we always meet on your side of the street, don't we?"

The Chairman, visibly distressed, cinched up his tie in a show of courage and whimpered, "Well, maybe this time we don't print off the extra money to buy your pork."

The Speaker leaned over to the Chairman, inching closer until the tips of their noses touched, and warned, "And now, as we stand on your side of the street, I'll quietly remind you a majority of Congress and the President of the United States of America signed these receipts. The President has the power to fire you, which I'm already encouraging him to do. Now, go display your independence and loan us the money for the Treasury debt the market won't buy." Pausing to regain an admiring demeanor, he finished. "And you know as well as I do, our existence as we know it, depends on spending more money than the taxpayers send us."

The Chairman, deflated and reprimanded, returned to the gilded dungeon of the Federal Reserve. Shackled to the loan default he'd allow, he thought of his counterpart, the Treasury Secretary, turning a big crank in debasement—sheets of paper worth trillions shooting into a tray. He'd have to mop up the debt not bought on the world's bond markets, and wring it out into a hidden bucket of worthless dollars.

So much fiat money flowed, it was bound to make its way to some unexpected places. Covered in the small print of the spending, a Cuban artist received a humanitarian grant to express his feelings about poverty. With a flare of creativity, he used a unique medium for his craft—fish hooks. The creation was so unusual, it was showcased in a most conspicuous place—the Art Show in Miami.

Anthony, a Wall Street buyer, lounged in an art deco chair. It was made of orange fabric stretched over aluminum rods and bent in the shape of a woman's hair clip. His legs fell uncomfortably through the teeth. He carefully positioned his gaze in front of the mural of soldered fishhooks resembling a stormy sea. Breathing in every nuance of the crashing canvas, the buyer began to mark the painting for market. He attracted the attention of the art dealer, smiled and said, "I'm Anthony. They call me the Rookie." Value needed unlocking and, as is unique to the art market, what you see is never all that you buy.

Thousands of tiny points and barbs sloshed around a small canoe made of two barbs meant for a shark and connected at both eyes. Plastic trash, melted into crumpled balls, dotted the mural as icebergs. The art dealer was herself a creation. She wore a gold bolero rimmed in dangling purple puff balls and a ravishing purple silk cropped jacket of a matador, trimmed in a feminine cut. Amplifying the moral ambiguity of the deal, her diamond necklace drooped between the open collar of her gold satin blouse, and the tight cut of her capri pants pulled the gold vertical stripes snug to her thighs. She turned toward the mural and with the one hand on her lithe hip, relished the provenance. "The trash was collected from the floating vortexes of garbage submerged in our oceans." For all that art money knew, the trash could've come from the drag bar on Ocean Blvd—but the back story increased the value. It was the same with fiat money. Its value depended on the country of origin along with the face painted on the front.

Anthony sipped on a glass of wine, distracted by the art dealer's bouncing purple puff balls. In an effort to sound knowledgeable on something he knew nothing about, he said, "I'm looking for something that will hold its value. I'm diversifying away from stocks and bonds."

The dealer's smile exposed her glee. She let her hand fall from her hip as she turned to face him. She looked into his eyes. "Tell me, Rookie. Do you know any of the owners of those companies? Do you know what they do?"

He shifted in his chair. "I don't have to know. I read last quarter's results. They come in the mail." Slightly embarrassed by his underestimation of the dealer's agency, and a little shaken from her ampleness which held back her diamonds, he shrugged. "It didn't go so well."

"Charming," she replied. Assuming the role as the broker of a transaction, she turned back toward the painting. She examined the mural and lit up with excitement. She talked to the stormy sea. "The man who assembled these hooks into the masterpiece before you is expressing his relentless poverty in Cuba." The puff balls bounced with every word. "The mural represents the relationship between the symbolic meaning of inanimate objects and the human psyche."

Mesmerized by her explanation and her bull fighting outfit, Anthony exclaimed, "I'll take it!" And at that moment, the power went out, and not just to the gallery, but to the entire city.

Attached to his stock and bond money like an addict to the syringe, the Rookie fidgeted as he pecked on his phone. "I can't access my bank account," he complained. Time sped up as the darkness fell outside the museum windows. The streets began filling with pandemonium. Looters flooded into the gallery, ripping art from the easels. Exasperated from unsuccessful attempts on his cell phone, Anthony was off the rails now with embarrassment and panic. He screamed, "My money's gone!" Dodging the human chaos around the booth, he crammed his phone in his jacket and jumped behind the orange art deco chair.

The art dealer's eyes flashed back and forth. She turned to the Rookie and shouted, "I must ask you to exit the booth. Volatility is on the march." And with the official release from his bargain, the Rookie bolted to the parking deck, found his car undamaged, and promptly drove out of town.

The art dealer, a veteran haggler and sharp shooter, readied herself for new buyers climbing through the broken windows. She pulled a revolver from somewhere beneath her matador jacket. She would not be deterred by a minor setback like revolution in the streets. Several looters approached her booth with ill intentions. "You'll die for these pieces, but the price is right," she bellowed through clenched teeth.

The looters looked at one another and proceeded to consider the dealer's offer. Art money's ticket was punched when, in return for a pocket of fiat money, the lead looter said, "We'll take all the big ones, and especially that one with the fish hooks. We can use the canvas for curtains and the frames for structure. The hooks we don't use, we can melt into bullets."

"Sold!" the dealer announced. She pocketed their fiat money in the same fold of her jacket where the revolver had been stored and relinquished the art money. The looter's new asset, masquerading as capital, went out the door painted on a couple of fakes and a burlap bag covered in fishhooks, soldered by a poor guy in Cuba.

Without agenda, mission, or passion, money transformed. Money was never influenced or prodded by euphemisms of weight—"Hey, big money!"—or amorous intention—"I love money." If it had mattered to money, but it didn't, the worst was the brutish jab of dirty money. But the sting doesn't linger when you're constantly getting cleaned and layered. Money valued everything of man's folly from costliest to cheapest—product, labor, and metal, in that order.

The fishhook art was escorted down the darkened Miami Strip, the tiny barbs in the sloshing sea pricking the looters' hands. They used the plastic icebergs as handholds. The investment plan didn't include a reserve for the tropical heat, as the painting slipped from their sweaty hands every few feet and banged on the sidewalk. The canvas loosened in the frame, and the fishhooks dropped off with every crash landing. Art money was becoming a liability.

As the looters rounded the corner, one surmised that his budding criminal career was yoked to the mediocrity of his gang. His bleeding fingertips and his wife's need of home improvement convinced him to divest. He decided an asset sale to satisfy his spouse was better than the extra labor involved in selling the art, framing artwork houses, or arming riflemen with fish hooks melted into bullets. In a moment of inspiration, he sold his portion of the spoils to the other two. Now, fiat Money hopscotched the international scene as it flew on a plane to Mexico, changed its name to peso, and bought a concrete driveway.

As commodity money hardened and became a driveway, labor money was pushed into global flow. Boozer, the driveway contractor's foreman, was an expat from the states on absence-without-a-leave from the US Army. He collected the workers to discuss their worth. "I promised each of you 1,000 pesos for one day, and we finished early. So, 800 pesos."

The leader of the crew, obviously with some skills and experience in labor representation, cried foul. "That's insane. We want a pension, too."

"A pension? Labor is half of my cost already. Will you take less money, if I include a retirement plan to attract and retain competent employees?"

The labor representative pressed his perceived advantage. "We could've worked a whole day anywhere else in town for 1,200 pesos. We could've collected 2,000 pesos in America for the same work, and received free healthcare."

Boozer responded with a trump card. "Well, go sell your children, buy a train ticket and make a run for the border, paco. There're ten guys here asking for your job every morning." Labor money was valued and split amongst the crew.

From his hefty management split, Boozer took his fiat money and found a cocaine trafficker. Every Friday afternoon he dialed up the same guy, and his fiat money became drug money.

Taking Boozer's advice, the labor representative jumped into action. But misunderstanding, he sold his casa instead of his children. With the diminished earnings, he bought a train ticket to the border, but the whole family had to ride on top or hang off the side.

The following week, Boozer hired two to replace the one. The new hires finished the job, and labor money settled into a pool of equilibrium at the barbeque Saturday afternoon. His drug money was invested in a cocaine plant, then wrapped in plastic and sent north to the border, too, but welded into car doors.

Drug money prayed for a quick end. Once at the Mexican-US border, it marveled in wonder at the quadrupled fiat Money packed into eighteen wheelers headed south in the opposite direction. Drug Money would never spread, multiply or grow. It would only get cut, sniffed and blown, then flushed into a swirling whirl of mortality down a porcelain black hole.

Watching drug money and fiat money traverse across land, petrol money sneered, dripping in oily crude. It was sailing out of port in a tanker ship. Never one to wallow in semantics, petrol money was the essence of liquidity. It cruised around the world, avoiding the missiles of diplomacy. Its mere existence protected by the hull of the boat. Its portability, reliability and unlimited access trumped all the tormented barrages of short-sighted environmental advocates. They were smooth talkers who couldn't see over the horizon to the safe harbors of the Far East. Confident of its need, petrol money sailed the seven seas while it laughed at the manmade desire for energy from sunshine and wind—neither of which could be saved or stored.

Back at the Mexican concrete company that had supplied the driveway, the remainder of pesos landed on the operational balance sheet as more fiat money. It grew restless and bored with accountability. But a hot streak flared, and fiat money caught a break. It found action in the finance department's overnight cash markets. Churning with decimals, it was discharged from the Western hemisphere riding on a transatlantic cable travelling at light speed. Riding the financial red-eye, fiat money went through more changes than dollars-to-chips in Vegas.

With a stop in Brussels, the peso transformed into a yen, a franc, and a pound; it pushed on an ethernet cable twisting through the bond markets of Tokyo, Zurich, and London. Through the corridors of world power, fiat money snaked through vaults full of gold money (petrol money's underground cousin, but with more polish and less energy).

Gold money was stacked in columns. It wore its value on its guns and jets and rockets.

In the presence of gold money, the earth shifted under fiat money, faced with its own bottomless downside of distrust. Fiat money felt intimidated, untethered to anything solid, its value backed by the dealers using it and nothing more. It had an epiphany that its only value lay in it being a better option than killing for food. After another sleepless night of international wire travel, fiat money shot back across the Atlantic and fell into a pool of dollars on Wall Street. It was 9:30 a.m., and the market opened.

The morning brought some clarity, and the liquidity of a Treasury pool. Fiat money felt the peculiar DNA of something new. It was like a hangover, but more viral. Suddenly, fiat money felt the flashy flamboyance of crypto money tingling across its face. It felt invincible and invigorated!

Stowing away along the overnight dark routes, crypto money had hidden among the block chains. It lurked in the blind spot of the bureaucrat's eroding power. Like a ghost, crypto money floated in the back alleys of the global persona non grata—places where fiat money, and its regulatory scent, were forbidden. And now crypto money was on the cusp of infecting the whole system. The bureaucrat's only hope for fiat money lay in crypto's limited volume.

Crypto money yearned for acceptance, but bore the brunt of regulation meant to hobble. Those shackles melted in the August heat as crypto money underwent a transformation. Every ham-handed slam of the bureaucrat's mallet splattered crypto money on vaults around the world in a rainbow of nationalities. Over time, crypto money learned the lesson of small numbers: No one listens until you have large numbers. Crypto money needed economies of scale; and fast.

Longing to rid the lingering taint of revolving electronic wallets, crypto money saw its chance. It slipped in the deep end of the Wall Street pool of dollars when fiat money grew lazy. Swirling with fiat money from around the world, it tried to gain some leverage in stacks of ones. Crypto had a brilliant idea. It suggested a game of liar's poker to the pool. Unfortunately for crypto, fiat money was subservient to its creator, the Federal Reserve, who lavishly hand cranked it into debasement. And there were no liars in the bunch. Crypto gasped as fiat money shunned it. All the ones jumped into a stack of numerical order according to each of their serial numbers. Sure, there were a few dollars, beguiled by the attraction of adventure, that joined in league with Crypto. But only enough to be tagged as an anomaly by the compliance department. Faster than a request denial from management, crypto money was swiped into a contra account and disappeared.

The pool of fiat money, stacked in ones and decimals, poured into the Rookie's hedge fund that he managed from a computer connected to his car phone. The Rookie was flush. Time to make some change. He bought shares in a technology company, a hospital, and a bar. The tech company he bought for investment return, the hospital for his health and the bar for his soul.

In an Irish accent, the Rookie's priest reminded him of money's embedded tracking device: "Follow your treasure, lad, and you will find your heart." So, he hedged his bar bet and presented his church with a gift of new offering plates. Money flowed.

It flowed through fat digital pipes and hand-to-hand contracts, through the borders of countries like wind, changing to suit the transaction. Like a river swollen from a rainstorm, the deep parts were slow and methodical, and the flood-ravaged banks muddy with the primordial ooze of innovation.

Money was enlightened by world travel, multiplied by business genius, and sanctified by charitable giving. Fiat money gathered itself on a tax return and took a trip back to Washington DC for the annual census, where it was shredded.

LEVERAGE

No one saw it coming. The stock market dropped through an elevator shaft—the biggest down week in history. Anyone with real money was poorer by half and desperate to get out, no matter the collateral damage.

Trudging through the icy wind blowing from the Hudson, I walked north on Broadway against the human herd marching south to Wall Street. The sharp corners of the towering skyscrapers groaned against the gusts. Brokers and bankers, shoed in black patent leather, marched in their worsted wool battle armor of fading prosperity. They tried to shield their pride from the day's coming dreary servitude. Gloom and snow clouds darkened my vision. The biting wind pushed at my carefully gelled black hair and froze the tip of my strong Italian nose. My chest tightened as I thought about the presentation I was about to deliver, having never had a margin call meeting before.

I darted across the blundering herd into Habib's. I decided to seek financial refuge in a few mega-lotto tickets. I supplemented my player's chance with aspirin and coffee in a feeble attempt to assuage the economic carnage.

I bumped into a lady on my way inside the store. She switched her eyes at me and then slipped on a small ice patch. Catching herself, she yelled at me sideways, "Watch it, rookie! Some of us have to be at work on time." I waved my apology and swung Habib's glass door open. Under the bright fluorescent lights, the door's electronic bell rang like a cash register; cha-ching.

"Habib! Coffee. Black. Aspirin, too, and three Mega Lottos."

"Sure thing, Tony," Habib said to me across the top of customer's heads. He handed change to them through the window. "You feeling lucky, Boss?" Habib called me boss because I wore a suit.

Stopping momentarily at the Lotto counter, I filled out three tickets. "I'm diversifying my portfolio." I used my wife's birthday, my son's birthday, and my dad's. I prayed over the mega lottos quickly and incomprehensibly. "Heavenly Father Almighty...whisper, whisper, whisper—so that I may have peace, prosperity and good will—whisper, whisper, whisper—Amen!" I poured coffee from the stained pot and pulled some money from the ATM for shoe-shiner stock tips and lunch. The whole store was smaller than my tiny Tribeca kitchen.

The check-out line was filled with haunting laughter, disguising the contagious fear rippling through the financial district. I stepped up to the counter and shoved my lotto tickets under the glass. Habib took them and returned an aspirin package. He dutifully asked, "How you doing?"

"Nothing new," I replied. "Same as yesterday and just as shitty."

Habib shook his head and asked empathetically, "Did you get out before the drop, Boss?" He leaned back in a watchman's posture to check the security screens under the cigarettes. The black and white quadrants shaping the outside of the store were in constant motion. He looked back at me with a grin, stroking his cat whiskers of a goatee. When I didn't answer, he punched up the register and said, "Eight fifty."

"Wise guy, huh," I said.

"Wise as you. If you win the lotto, I get ten percent. All I have to do is show up and pay the rent. No one's going to rip me off. I got cameras." He scanned his screens again, his suggestion of my vocation's goal hanging in the air.

I pushed a ten-dollar-bill under the glass and said, "You know, I build portfolios you don't have to sell, right?"

"You can't have my business, Tony. I don't use stock brokers. I trade online," he said through the window, ending a conversation I hadn't started. He scanned my tickets into the lotto database. "Do you tell your rich clients how you beat the lotto every day? Or is it just me watching you lose your highly-educated money?" He handed me a dollar-fifty in change.

"Habib, you work in this shoebox of a store. Haven't you ever wanted to drop it all and move away?"

He leaned back and looked into the screens. "Where am I going? I love it here." An epiphany struck him, and he turned to me. "So. Let me guess. You didn't get out before the drop?" He folded his arms and scratched the short hairs of his cat whiskers. "Well, I did. I've been sitting on some cash."

"You mean the cash leftover from those broke pot-stocks I told you not to buy?" I grabbed my coffee, turned, and walked past the ATM and the lotto counter.

He laughed and shouted as I reached the door, "Hey, Boss. I love my job! I'm lucky that way. Just let me know when your models say it's time to buy."

"Now." I tried to slam the door. It hesitated in the grip of a gas operated door closer. Finally, it closed behind me with an electronic cha-ching, but not before Habib's mocking laughter escaped through the gap.

My predicament sank in. My manager called my upcoming compliance-mandated meeting with Bishop David a workout—one I'd have to lead. David had always called our meetings "chapel," where he led. In my briefcase was the world's best research, circles sliced into pie shapes filled with fruitful colors, spit out of the printer before I'd left the office. The performance bar chart showed climbing piles of money, except for the last bar in the row. It created a cliff shape. How could I be blamed? Surely Bishop Dave would understand.

I ripped the aspirin package open, popped them in the back of my throat, and chased them with coffee. I threw the wrapper in a trash can next to a hot dog vendor. He was loading a brat for a homeless guy. Standing straight up with tongs in one hand and the open bun in the other, he spoke up from behind me.

"Hey Hollywood! You can't afford sanitation service at your dump in Jersey? Keep your headaches to yourself. You hear me, asshole!?" I hustled along, a dull pounding filling my head.

I shuffled through the oncoming crowd, a block away from my meeting. A swinging wrecking ball caught my attention just before it crashed into the side of a building. The shapes of bomb craters dotted the building's face, as dust and glass exploded off a third-story balcony. The swinging ball's momentum put a bend in the cable. I paused and watched as the ball landed another direct hit. Like an ancient warrior's battle sling, the fist of progress punched into the future.

Avoiding the taxis and buses zig-zagging through the street, I stopped at the crosswalk. My eyes rested on Bishop Dave's orphanage and my childhood home. He housed lost children like I once was, and owned the entire corner of real estate. On the opposite corner of the intersection standing like a refuge for the weary was Bishop Dave's cathedral.

Men and women in suits stood erect in the crowded buses, and swung from metal bars as the light turned green, their faces buried in newspapers. The steam from the manhole covers and bus exhaust engulfed the intersection.

Across the street and squeezed in between office towers was a small café, The Daily Grind. Dave and my time-honored rendezvous, it was famous for its on-site butchered meat. The strong coffee and gambling scene were added benefits.

As the light turned red, a mechanical computer voice on the corner told me it was safe to cross. A flood of traffic stopped in both directions. Bowing my head and holding both lapels in one hand and my briefcase in the other, I marched into the wind. I passed two rows of hood ornaments, and a third stopped within inches of my briefcase. "Dammit, man. I've got the light!" I shouted.

The cabbie clobbered his horn. Above the wail of his

late model yellow cab, he leaned out the window and yelled, "Well hurry up, suit!"

The wrecking ball kept knocking on the condemned building on the intersection's last corner. The strikes were hitting my temples, too. I finally arrived at the bottom steps of the The Daily Grind and stepped into "chapel".

I passed through the front door of the diner. Just inside was Bishop Dave who I recognized by the red zucchetto on his head. Plastering a confident smile on my face, I slid in the booth. "Hello, Bishop Dave! It's been a while." I dragged the toboggan off my head and dropped it on my briefcase in the window casement. We enjoyed a front row view of the wrecking ball across the street. I picked up the plastic menu laying on the white linoleum table top.

In his rector's Irish accent, he opened the show. "Hello, lad. This isn't confession. It's just chapel and breakfast." His eyes came to rest on me without hesitation, agenda, or pre-conception. "I'm always glad to meet with our orphanage's graduates. Especially one that's done so well managing God's money. Money God made me steward over." His grey eyes gleamed, the rounded lines of his jaw still set square under the layers of age. The wrinkles on his forehead folded above his bushy eyebrows.

I said, "Well, I have good news. I haven't lost it all." I chuckled, but he didn't. The financial reports in my bag told a different story. "If the government wouldn't waste so much money," I continued, "they wouldn't need the Federal Reserve to pull them from the ditch every ten years."

Dave rubbed the bottom of his nose back and forth. I turned away to let him reflect on what I'd said. I watched the looping arcs of the wrecking ball out the window. The façade it was pounding reminded me of a lotto ticket, with the holes like the dark bubbles of number selections circled in with pencil. My head pounded with the rhythm. Dave yawned.

I blathered on. "I beat the market out of dimes, and The Fed flushes it with trillions. Why bother? Just put it all on red, bet the house and never look back. No harm with that strategy, right? The government will feed the bull every time that mean ole' bear comes sniffing around."

If he had checked his account online, the losses certainly didn't show on Dave's face. He pointed through the glass to the demolition and said, "Anthony, do you know how to operate a wrecking ball?"

"No," I said.

"Well, neither do I. Like you, I already have a job. God blessed me with a full cathedral yesterday. First time in ten years. Whether the markets go up or down, my portfolio is hedged."

The candy-striped waitress came over to take our orders. She shifted her weight to one foot. "Bishop, the usual?"

"That's right, Angelica. Surprise me." She shook her head as she wrote.

Smiling, she asked me, "What're you having?"

"Burger. Rare. And another coffee."

She stopped writing and looked at me. "Do you want any fries, or just a burger, rare?"

"That's it. No fries. Doctor's orders."

She dropped her smile, then her pad and pen to her

sides "You picked the wrong place to come with a doctor's note. Back in a minute," she said with a smirk. The meat grinder behind the counter whirred to life, and the smell of cooking hash and eggs filled the room.

"Before you go, Angelica, this is Anthony. He's one of our first orphans from our earliest days. Now he's our banker. An acquired taste, but smart."

"Whatever you say, Bishop." She stood on her back foot and put the hand with the note pad on her hip. "What do you think about the new orphanage, Anthony?"

"What new orphanage?" I asked. Dave didn't change his expression of innocent engagement.

"Right across the street from your orphanage, where the wrecking ball is doing a number on that apartment building," she said with the omnipotence of inside knowledge. "Bishop Dave will own all four corners on this block once his church buys us out, too."

I shifted in my seat. "That'd be great," I said, and then added, "Are you the owner?"

"Yep, and I'm about to move to Florida. So, no, thank you for your help," she said, her gaze hurling daggers at mine. Walking back to the coffee pot, Angelica braked before she was knocked about by a bulldozer of a man in a black leather jacket and big shoes. "Watch your step, Louie!" she shouted.

"What's wrong with her?" he asked the room, his thumb pointing behind him. He bulldozed over to our booth. A big nose poked from the middle of his potato face and his head was covered with short black hair. His hands were as big as baseball gloves. They flailed around the hinges of his wrists. One came up and slapped David on the back. "Bishop Dave, how you doin'?" he asked. "Youse' ready to make some real money? Kierkegaard's Possibility is three-to-one across the board. You could pair that with an exacta. Take Kirk to win and First-Chance-Last-Chance to place. My guy in the paddock told me they're the only two ponies in the race that dope. I feel good about it."

Still reconciling the Brooklyn brogue of his last words, my jaw muscles clenched with the understanding of his offer.

"Morning, Louie. Anthony is my banker." Dave barely raised his hand from the table, gesturing to me.

"Oh. Hey, Pal," he said over the diner's bustle.

"Hey." I raised a napkin to wipe my brow. The cold air rushed through the door and steamed on my throbbing forehead. "Louie, is it?"

"Yea, Louie," he said and paused. "Look, paisan. Don't take no offense, but you look like dried dogshit on concrete—waiting for rain so you can stink again."

"I'll be fine. Thanks for your concern, Lou." I crumpled the napkin in my fist. The tension in my chest riveted my eyes in the cool resting place of Dave's.

"It's Louie, with an "e", and you're welcome," he said. He looked back to Dave and spoke again, "I'll be over here runnin' my game at the back table. Let me know if you want in."

"I like Kierkegaard's Possibility to win. Bet the house," Dave replied.

Louie's hands began to twirl, "You're on, Bishop." A broad smile spread across Louie's face as he turned and lumbered to a back table. He was surrounded by squares posing as high rollers. While calling in Dave's wager, his free hand reached into his pocket, retrieving a deck of cards.

Dave looked at me and said, "It's not the things we don't know that get us in trouble, Anthony. It's the things we're certain are true, but aren't."

I began to reply, "I know," but I didn't. More immediately, I needed to uncover the origin of Dave's new orphanage financing, so I went with, "Where'd you get the money to buy the apartment complex and this place?"

"From the money on our first loan," he said, and preened the lapels of his clerical collar. "Where else?"

Shocked and still not comprehending why Dave would consider a bank contract negotiable, I said, "That money was for your parish's pensions. What am I going to tell my manager?"

I was dizzy with the rumble from my gut. Out the window, I saw the wrecking ball slam headlong into a long straight hallway. The taught cable ripped a deep void into the core of the building and hung up in the building's framework. The operator jerked the cable through the floors of the building, causing the ball to crash into each higher ceiling. After several more violent jerks of the ball, the crane began to come off the ground. Eventually, the ball released itself to swing freely again.

Angelica came back with our coffee and put the cups in front of us. Dave stirred his cup and placed the spoon back on the rim of the saucer. "Like the wrecking ball guy, Anthony, I don't know your business. Please tell your manager we're thankful for the loan. It will make a beautiful new orphanage. And this place? This place is going to be wonderful. We're building a women's center around the Grind, keeping the restaurant and butcher shop intact."

"Apologies for the interruption." Angelica dropped the plates on the tables with enough momentum that they slid in front of us. My burger bled onto the plate, leaving the meat gray. Dave's lips separated with a glorious smile. He proclaimed, "Hash and eggs. My favorite! Thank you, Angelica. You're too good to me."

She tucked her chin in her shoulder and said, "You're welcome, Dave." She turned back to the next table while letting me know in faux hospitality, "If you need any ketchup for your burger, it's on the counter."

My shirt buttons felt like they were popping. I went back to business. "What about your pensions?"

"Please. The church is strong. Our servants serve God. Not the God of money, but the God of Peace. Their pensions are paid. We borrowed money from your bank because we're proud of you, and you asked us to."

My face flushed as I reached for my bag and pulled out the charts. "Dave, we need to talk about the pension loan. You've got a margin call on your private account."

He sipped his coffee again. "What's a margin call?"

I walked him through the rising charts of financial success in the early days, years ago. Ruffling through to the last pages, early success metamorphosed into a graphical cliff face of steep losses, the impetus of the margin call. I pointed to the minus sign and said, "You borrowed money against your stocks. I told you if the market dropped, you'd have to sell stocks to pay the difference in the collateral amount and the loan." Dave removed his zucchetto and placed it on the seat beside him. Legally required to explain, I continued, "To meet the call, I have to sell some of your stocks or get a personal check from you."

His head bowed, he whispered aloud and quietly, "... to our use, And thus to thy service - whisper, whisper, whisper—grateful praise, amen." Two-handed, he re-placed the zucchetto on his head, forked a helping of hash, and looked at me with friendly eyes. Quietly, they closed in buttery hash comfort. Before opening them again and, seemingly, levitating he chewed through his questions, "Are you suggesting we sell stocks at the bottom of a stock market bust? Is that wise?"

"Unless you can pull money from some other place, I have to."

"Okay, I'll send you money from the cash reserves left-over from the pension loan we're using for the apartment complex being torn down, and the Grind. It'll be a week or two, though. We've had some planning issues come up that need the blessing of a councilman. As you know, smooth-ing these things over cost money."

"I repeat, Dave: that money is for your pensions. And it wouldn't matter anyway." I lowered my head. "I need the money today or tomorrow."

David wiped his mouth with a napkin and asked, "It is a confusing job you have, isn't it?" He gulped his coffee and scooped another bite of hash and eggs. Talking around the food, he said, "Tell you what. If I can't pay down the margin call in two weeks, then we can't make the payment on the pension loan you suggested."

I slowly shook my head. "It doesn't work that way, either, Dave."

The wrecking ball took a wide circling arc and bashed in the back of the building. Then it came blasting through the front side and headed straight for our booth window, only to curl back around in mid-air under the rotating crane boom.

Attentive to my body language, he asked, "Would you like me to pray for you, Anthony? Louie was right. You don't look so good." He removed his zucchetto again and placed it to the side and began to pray, "Heal us, Lord, if it is your will—whisper, whisper, whisper—You are the giver of Life—whisper, whisper, whisper".

Frustrated, I stopped his praying. "I'd like you to stop gambling so I wouldn't have to tell my only real father that I have to sell all his stocks at the bottom of the stock market. And I'd like you to tell me you're going to use your pension loans to pay the church pensions and you're not going to pay for—what did you call it?—smoothing things over with a councilman? You're going to own all four intersections!?" I shoved my bloody hamburger to the side and dabbed the crumpled napkin to my forehead again. When I pulled it from my face, Dave came up from a bow, gesticulated, and put the zucchetto back on his head, two-handed.

"Since you mentioned it, how is your father, Anthony? Remember when we found him? Oh, what a reunion."

"Yes, Dave. I'm grateful. Now he lives with us, thinks my wife is his girlfriend, and I'm breaking into his house when I come home. It's a lot."

Dave finished his hash and eggs and asked, "What'll you do, Anthony? About my pension loan, I mean?"

"Well, it'll be the worst-case scenario. My bank will sue your church."

Dave wiped his hands. "Really? You're going to sue a church for paying our pensions, building a new orphanage and a women's center? Do you think the Times will want to interview me?" He laughed out loud as he used to when he beat me at chess. It felt as if we were playing a new game now. "C'mon, Anthony. Liar's poker for the bill, for ole' time's sake."

Exhausted from Dave's mental gymnastics and reinvigorated by the sense of optimism I felt from risk, I pulled out the dollar in change from Habib's. "Ok, three aces."

"Big bluffer from the start, eh? I'm holding four aces, so I'll bet five aces."

Knowing Dave's penchant for subtlety, I said, "Six aces," unknotting my tie. Perspiration seeped through my shirt sleeves with every throb of my temples and the extra cup of coffee wasn't helping.

"No way. Show me," he called. I flipped the dollar over between my fingers revealing the serial numbers; no zeros, or aces as we called them. Dave turned his over revealing three. As he bent over the table to examine my dollar, his eyes widened and he said, "Seems you don't hold any aces today, Anthony." He sipped his coffee and bragged. "Knew it. Breakfast on you." He smiled his warm smile.

Angelica dropped the bill in front of me without knowing about our wager. Louie yelled from the back table ringed with suckers, "Full House! Ladies over Jacks. Beat that!" The pigeons folded their cards as Louie raked the pile.

Dave waited as I paid Angelica at the register. Louie came up behind us. "Tony, you look even worse," he said.

I shoved the leftover bills Angelica gave me into my wallet. Turning to Louie, I saw the falling wrecking ball behind him plunge into the only floor remaining. It dropped like an apple from a tree and crashed with a thud to the ground floor. The vibration from the flattened rubble rippled across the street to where we stood.

My heart stopped. Losing consciousness, I fell to the white tile. My wallet fell to the floor before me. I lay there, unable to move. Life spun in my head. My real father lived in my house with my wife and didn't know the president's name. My adopted father was someone I didn't know, and my bank wasn't going to get paid. The last thought limping through my mind was, too late now.

Louie reached down and pressed two fingers to my neck. I heard him say, "Wow, Dave. He's dead. Not his lucky day."

Dave said, "In baptism, he died with Christ—whisper, whisper, whisper—May he share in his fullness in death."

Louie checked my pockets. "Do you want these lotto tickets?" he looked up and asked Dave.

Dave said, "Heavens, no. I never gamble with other people's money. Leave that and his wallet for his family. Maybe they can enjoy them for Christmas."

STITCHES

It was the year before Dad died on a deserted two-lane county highway. Mom drove him back and forth to the hospital, so occasionally she unloaded my brother James and me on Uncle Peter—Pete for short. My name's John. Mom named us after two brothers in the Bible. She told us they were called the "Sons of Thunder". Uncle Pete didn't have kids, nor was he married, nor did he lead a life we knew anything about.

On our maiden voyage on the USS Uncle Pete (that's what he called our visits), we set sail on a fall afternoon on the way to one of Dad's many doctor appointments. With James and I in tow, mom opened Pete's screen door and welcomed our family into the house. Uncle Pete was seated in a recliner in the front room. He didn't look up when the door opened. The brown and blue stripes of his plaid short-sleeve shirt went with his curly hair and eyes. Pete's forearm muscles pulsed and his hand manipulated the contents in the brown paper bag on his lap. On his arm was a tattoo of a fuzzy globe, stabbed by an anchor with an eagle on top. Pulling out a handful of peanuts, he crushed the shells and dropped them on the floor. Finally noticing us, he popped a couple of nuts in his mouth and talked through his crunching, "Hey, sis. You boys find a spot anywhere."

James caught me off guard with a gut-punch. He mumbled, "Don't mess with anything, John," as he skirted around the bear rug. His braces added a lisp to his s's. James threw my plastic bag of clothes and toothbrush on the oldest recliner he didn't prefer. Then he tossed his own onto the newer version next to Uncle Pete. Hurting, I rubbed my ribs as I planned my counter attack.

Mom stood in the open door, beautiful in her cream-colored cotton dress and her curly brown hair—a feminine match of Uncle Pete's. She asked about the new recliners. Uncle Pete said he'd stolen them at Huck's Furniture & Gun Shop. Mom replied, "No surprise, there. I saw the clearance sign last week." Then she kissed us both on the cheek. "Your Uncle Pete has Gordon's authority." (That was our dad's name.) "See that you use it, Pete," mom said.

"They're not my problem." Uncle Pete said with a grin—probably because he got away with stealing the chairs. James and I never got away with anything.

Hands on her hips, Mom gave her best Billy Graham impersonation, dropping her divine words on Pete and his bag of peanuts. "The Lord doesn't give someone more than they can handle." Then she leaned over and hugged him, thanking him again and walked out. The screen door creaked closed. She shouted back. "Don't let them get away with anything!" Uncle Pete continued eating peanuts and watching baseball. Mom climbed in her Buick and shut the car door with a bang. Dad sat in the passenger seat. The dust spewing from underneath her back tires clouded the front yard as she pulled away.

My brother and I started roaming the house unattended. We found bedrooms on the sides of the main hallway. They were all a treasure trove of family pictures. In the back room there was a dining table with eight sides like a stop sign, and a fuzzy top. It had grooves on all of the edges that I could push my toy cars in. On the table were stacks of red, white and blue plastic coins. It had cup holders, too. Stacked in the corner were gloves with sleeves and metal helmets with sunglasses that looked a lot like work. In the next corner, a heavy metal box was labeled with the word "safe". Rods and reels leaned in a third corner. Those were leaning next to a couple of long guns with little tubes at the ends. On a table by itself sat plates full of bullets, stacked on top of one another. Bolted on that table was a machine with a lever and an upside-down soda bottle stuck in the top, full of black shiny flakes. Mom told us Uncle Pete was a special kind of hunter; said "he'd hunt evil anywhere in the world it tried to hide". That's why he was gone so much.

From where James and I stood, we looked out the back of the house through three big windows. There was Pete's truck, with metal boxes saddled on each side of the bed. Beyond that was a metal roof supported by telephone poles shading old, rusty tractors. Twisty tree limbs from the creek bank leaned against the poles. Animal horns and skulls hung on the walls nailed to the side poles. Out past the truck and Uncle Pete's stuff was open farmland as far as I could see.

Our temporary house sniffed out, we made our way back to the front room and plopped down in the stolen recliners. It was then I noticed the animal heads across all four walls caught in a stare. Two bass mounted on a piece of wood next to the fireplace were bigger than anything down at Huck's Furniture and Gun Shop. The two biggest deer on the wall hung at the edge of the TV, forking up to the ceiling. When James asked who's they were, Uncle Pete replied, "Boone and Crockett." I assumed those two friends of Pete's had formed the butt shapes in our seats. Next to Mom and Dad's picture on the mantel was a photo of Uncle Pete and a pretty girl with the words High School Prom above them.

Mom not present and her warnings now a distant memory, I began my revenge on James' earlier assault while Uncle Pete and James watched a Thursday night college football game. At the commercial I asked. "What's in the barn out back?"

"My taxidermy shop," Pete said. "I mount deer heads and fish."

"Do you have a dog?"

"No. Too much trouble."

"Why do you have a bomb in your yard," I kept on. James glanced at me hard.

"No, not a bomb. That's a propane tank. It runs the heater and the stove."

"Did you and Mom live here when you were kids?"

"Yep. It was your grandfather's house. You finished?"

Annoyed by my questions, James added a balled-up fist to his stare, the signal I was looking for. Just one, maybe two more. "Is that a picture of your girlfriend?"

James throttled his recliner forward, propelling himself toward me screaming "You asked for it!"

I launched like a bobcat, my counter-attack meeting him in the middle of the room. He stepped to the side, raised his arm and clotheslined me at the neck. I landed flat on the bear-rug. As my head bounced up from the furry carpet, James flipped me over. My knuckles twisted behind my back as he bore his knee into my spine. My right hand was buried under my chest, driving the air from my lungs with every word James uttered. His knee bounced in time with each word. "Mom! Made! Him! Take! Us! He! Didn't! Ask! For! Us!" I snickered at his lisp, which only made him angrier. His braces raked my exposed ear lobe I'd hoped to save, with not much hope for the other buried in the rug. I inhaled the bear musk and boot dust puffing up from the floor.

Uncle Pete hollered out above the action. "Hey! Fight outside or fight me!" James came to attention. Allowing me up, he released his hold as if the whole thing never happened. His mood swings became worse as Dad got sicker.

Now I was just full of raw anger. I decided to break the one rule Dad made about fist fighting. Without warning I sucker-punched him right in the mouth. My fist slammed his lips to his teeth, stapling his face to his braces. Blood trickled from his mouth, his eyes watered and his face turned bright red. Uncle Pete's eyes iced over with disapproval.

Being older and nobler, James honored Dad's instructions by not punching me back. Instead, he swung his open palm at the end of his arm limb. I caught a glimpse of it out of the corner of my burning eye, but not soon enough to stop him from slapping me back to the ground.

I laid sprawled on the floor, one eye staring at the bear head attached to the rug, the other eye filled with Uncle Pete. He yanked his recliner forward bouncing his curly dark hair around his ears, his cheeks straining with wrinkles. I could feel him making noise, but couldn't hear anything. Uncle Pete raised his leg, and his boot came down hard with a thud and another cloud of dust. Just then, I felt a second thud behind me. Uncle Pete and James both froze. I pushed myself up to my knees and turned to see Boone's deer head laying on the floor, minus one antler. Crockett's deer head was still on the wall, but Boone's was broke up bad.

Uncle Pete walked over to the wall, picked up the broken bone and stuffed it in his back pocket. He gripped the deer's remaining antler, still connected to the head, with one hand and me under my armpit with the other. Spit slinging from his mouth, he contorted his head toward James while he took control of the moment. His voice filled the front room as the ringing in my ears died down and my hearing slowly returned: "...wah-wah-wah—if you don't fight outside, devil be damned!" He paused for a moment to look at me and furrowed his brows into a question mark. Then he shook my double vision into focus. "Get ice for your brother's lip! And your face! You both look wasp bit!" he ordered. He dropped my arm so I could obey. "James, sit on the couch and don't let others drive your boat. You're brothers, for Christ's sake." Uncle Pete walked out and slammed the screen door behind him, marching towards the antler filled shed behind the house.

I went to the kitchen and found a dish towel under

the sink and filled it with a handful of ice from the fridge. When I got back to the front room, James had made his way to the back room.

I struggled to follow, wondering where he'd hidden his boat, how long he'd kept it a secret from me and when he would let me drive it. I arrived a moment later and handed James the towel of ice as a peace offering. We both hid behind the metal box marked "safe" and watched Uncle Pete through the window. His shadow visible from the moonshine glowing off the cotton fields, he stopped to lean on the bomb-shaped propane tank, bowed his head and started talking to himself. I jumped for the door to ask Uncle Pete where he was going—but my collar tightened around my neck. James snatched the back of my shirt. "You're lucky I don't beat your ass again," he said, stopping me and spitting blood in my face.

I rolled my shoulder to pull loose and spoke in my defense. "It's not my fault."

He said what Dad had said many times, "The truth ain't in ya." That was usually followed by a suggestion of actual punishment. James, sounding a lot like dad, said, "You're about to learn taxidermy a lot sooner than you expected," the braces tripping up his words. He put the ice-filled towel up to his mouth. Silently I resolved to hold in my fight when I was at Uncle Pete's.

We spent quite a few nights at Uncle Pete's through the winter and early spring. Occasionally Pete would disappear on an out-of-town job from a few days to a week or more. Lucky for us, Uncle Pete was available one more time.

Dad shuffled to the car, his arm wrapped around Mom's shoulder on one side, James pushing at his hip on the other. We were on the road at dusk when Mom saw Uncle Pete's welding truck parked on the shoulder of the highway. In front of that truck was a farm plow and a tractor, parked in a way that looked like it was broken down. A farmer was smoking a cigarette over in the shade of a tree. The sun was setting on the other side of the half-plowed field behind dad, almost beaming through his thin silhouette in the passenger seat of the car.

Mom slowed down as we pulled up alongside Uncle Pete, his back to us while he welded on the plow. She turned to us in the back seat and said, "Get out." She leaned over to Dad's window knob and rolled it down, her extended arm circling in dad's lap, and yelled, "Pete!"

The sizzling arc on the end of the stick popped off. Uncle Pete tossed his welding helmet back. He turned around and looked at Dad in the front seat. I climbed out of the back seat on the highway side, and came around in time to see James standing outside Dad's window. Dad was slumped over. Uncle Pete grimaced. One of his hands, gloved to the elbow, came to rest on James's shoulder. Unable to move, I started to cry. Mom told us, "Don't worry. I'll see you later. Thanks, Pete."

He said, "I love you, Sis," his hand still on James' shoulder.

Mom's eyes watered. She spun the car sideways as she left us, making grooves in the high grass until the back tires lurched back onto the road. The engine roared as she drove away.

Uncle Pete tossed James a set of keys and told us to sit in his truck. Right before we got in, he said, "If you watch the welding, it'll blind you, and I'll know because you'll be blind." With that, he popped his dark helmet back over his face and bent back down to continue his work. I watched as the liquid metal dripped from white flame, immediately feeling my eyeballs scorch. Sitting in the floorboard of the truck, we could see the sparky glow above the dash. One of Uncle Pete's rock songs played on the radio. My eyes hurt and had dark spots where the welding flame had been. I had more questions than answers, and the only words James had was, "Shut up."

I started thinking about dad. Last weekend we came home from James' baseball game and stood next to the bed where dad lay. James quietly rubbed his home run ball in his hands. He'd hit a homer and got a loud cheer at the field but the thin smile dad made hearing the story meant more. Dad asked James if he could hold his ball. "I'm proud of you both. James, you gotta be the stitches holding this family together. John, mind your brother. I won't be here forever." I hung on dad's words as I sat on the floorboard of Uncle Pete's truck.

After a time, the welding light popped off. The truck cab darkened. The farmer cranked the tractor to life. He switched on its headlights that gave the inside of the truck a glow like a movie space ship. Uncle Pete began towing his red metal box toward the truck, which prompted James to jump out and pick up the wire cables dragging behind him. After loading up, we started down the dark highway. Uncle Pete answered my question I was too scared to ask. "I was arc welding the universal joint to the sheared shaft of that tractor so it could limp home, just like your mom's been doing for Gordon."

From my middle seat, I stared at the road with its dashed yellow lines flashing in the headlights, piecing together what I'd seen. James nudged me without turning away from the pitch-black window and gave the hard answer. "Dad went to heaven," he said. I cried again.

The following few days were a blur with mom, men in suits at the house talking quietly, going to the funeral home, lots of phone calls, more tears. The next Saturday, dad was buried in his blue suit. Mom cried at the funeral. Afterward she bustled around the house serving plates of food and talking to her church friends. Uncle Pete picked us up the following week to "give your mom some space," he said, even though she "didn't think it was necessary". James and I watched as he drove up the street and parked across from our little house. Mom was signing some papers on the hood of her car. The man with the papers didn't offer a tissue when she wiped her tears. Uncle Pete waited in his truck with his eyes straight ahead and his window rolled down. I leaned on mom's hips. James stood watch between mom and the man that took our house key from her. Mom explained to us, in a sad voice, that she'd sold the house.

Overjoyed to be leaving town, we scurried over to Uncle Pete and threw our stuff in the truck bed. Everything we owned was stuffed into a couple of grocery bags.

Mom put a baked ham in Uncle Pete's cooler, the browned-honey smell following us to his truck. His left arm hung out of the window, while his other rested on the steering wheel, his fingers tapping the dash.

James opened the passenger's side truck door, stood to the side and whispered, "Shotgun. You're riding bitsch' all the way there." Climbing into the middle, I made a mule-kick but missed the target. My heel flailed wide left as James inhaled across his braces. James' shoes banged on the running board as he jumped into Uncle Pete's truck. I had one hand on the seat buckle and the other on the dashboard. I swung my knees under me just in time to feel James' fingernails swipe air across my back.

Uncle Pete hollered, "Devil be damned! Can't you two leave each other alone for ten minutes!?"

James' eyes went wide. Having sailed on the USS Uncle Pete all winter long we were accustomed to his demands. We'd been scared straight, as mom hung her head. James pulled the door shut, rolled down the window and adjusted the over-sized side mirror. He swiveled his head in his reflection, "I hope you don't get braces 'til high school, jackass." I knew he meant me.

Mom laid her hands on the window's ledge of his truck and said, "All I have left are these two," a pair of her raised fingers pointing at us, "and the car."

Uncle Pete handed her a tissue from the glove box. "Well, I got 'em for a couple of days. Stay at the house as long as you need, or until you find a new place. That check should help," Pete said, pointing at the stack of pages the man had left her. "You know where everything is in case anyone comes around. Freezer's full and the guns are loaded."

As we drove away, Mom's image in the rearview mirror got smaller. I saw her waving good-bye and dabbing the tears from her cheeks. Her figure shrunk in the distance, framed by the two metal boxes on each side of the truck.

EMPTY BOAT SLIP

Spring rain cascaded through the swamp. You would only know Dead Lakes if you had seen the highway exit sign. The warning card hanging on the glass door of the bait shop read Do Not Feed the Alligators!

On the drive down, Uncle Pete told us to stay calm in the heat of anger. We minded him the whole trip. As a reward, James drove his own boat rented from the bait shop. We were coasting side by side in the canal. James captained his small ship, while I road in the front of Uncle Pete's. Small john-boats that looked exactly like ours were moored under make shift lean-tos along both banks. The owners slept dry in their cinder block cabins built by the water's edge.

"Can you rent me my own boat this afternoon?" I asked Uncle Pete.

"James earned it. You haven't," he said. Rain spattered his face.

James smiled at me from his boat and shouted back, "Thanks, Uncle Pete!" Still grinning with pride, he covertly shot me a bird with his middle finger laid over the side of the boat. Then the rain stopped and the sun came out. My red skin started to bake. I couldn't really retaliate against James. So I opted for daydreaming.

I dipped my fingertips in the water as the boat leaned

back and forth. We drifted along. Cypress tree stumps jutted out of the dark water. A massive black and white bird—osprey, I think?—set down in a tree not far away. Droplets fell from its wings back into the water. There were S-curves along the bank from water moccasins. That sight drew a response from Uncle Pete. "Pull your fingers in the boat." Just then an S-curve off the bow of our boat exploded in a splash. The snake was swallowed by a large fish and then the leftovers dropped back into the water. Drifting ahead I spotted a dark snout with a rock-shaped nose. It swirled and snapped under the surface as our boat neared his space. The rain had stopped, but a moment later it started again, and poured.

Uncle Pete flicked the switch to cut our motor. James did the same, copying Uncle Pete's every move. I braced for the waterfall ahead. Rainwater gushed off the metal roof of the camp lean-to onto our tiny boats. The water splashed off the boat, making its drumbeat on the aluminum bow, then me, then the turtle-shell gas tank, and ending on the outboard motor. My life jacket—the only one anybody was wearing—glued my shirt onto my sunburned back. We moved into the boat slips of the dock. As we bumped to a stop, my burnt skin caught fire.

James's docked his boat, stood, yawned and stretched. He had a swagger, his brown hair curling above his eyebrows, some fray on his cut-off blue jeans and rippling his shirt's wet stripes. He yanked his catch—a stringer of bream—from his live well and dropped them on the dock. Even the small vibration of fish hitting the wood caused me to flinch inside my life jacket, reigniting my sunburn. With some skill, he wrapped and knotted both our boat lines around a cleat on the dock.

Trying not to move in any way that made my sunburn sting, I sat perfectly still. Uncle Pete glared at me, wanting me to get out of the boat without saying anything. Still finding my legs, I pried my hands loose from the boat bench and crawled forward, holding on to anything solid. Uncle Pete called after me with a stern warning.

"Don't put your hand on a water moccasin," he said.

James gripped the strap of my life jacket and hauled me off the boat. I stood next to him on the dock. I tried to yank myself loose, but James tightened his grip just to mess with me.

Back by the outboard motor, Uncle Pete looked up at us. He was squatting down and his knees stuck out from under his armpits. He stood and winked. Without warning he started pedaling his feet up-and-down faster than one, two, three. Water splashed on the dock at our feet. Empty soda cans bounced around the boat's floor. It looked funny and we laughed at anything that didn't remind us of dad's funeral. The boat stilled beneath his feet. His cowboy hat was wet and the brim curved down from the weight of the water. The top scraped the rafters supporting the low metal roof. He bent over, flopped open the live-well lid, and pulled out two stringers of fish. The noose of the first cord threaded through the jaws of two largemouth bass, their feathery webbed tails dripped a fishing-line length of slime that hung just above the side of the boat. The cord in his other hand was much heavier, turning his fist white and coloring his fingers blood red. From it swung a bunch of fat shellcrackers, each the size of two of your hands laid flat and connected at the pinkies. He crowed with fisherman's pride, "That's what we're after, boys!" Looking over to us, he said, "James, put these with yours, and throw 'em on ice."

Uncle Pete unwrapped the cord from his hand. At the same time James wound it around his, gripping it hard as it was heavy to carry, reddening his fist. He threw the stringers of fish in the coolers by the cleaning-shack. Then he covered them with ice from the bait shop.

James and Uncle Pete took the cane poles from our boats and leaned the them in the corner of the dock. The rain slowed. Uncle Pete slung his cowboy hat down by his side, releasing a spray of raindrops splashing in the empty boat slip. He looked at James, "We're headed up to the cabin. It's too wet out here for boys. You coming?"

"No, sir," James said. I paused and turned to make sure I heard him right. Uncle Pete had given us the all-clear to take a nap. The morning was over. The honey-glazed ham mom sent was waiting for us in the cabin. "I'm not tired." I wasn't convinced. It sounded fishy.

Uncle Pete lowered his voice and leaned in, "Be careful around that bull gator. He's lurking out there somewhere." And with that, his wet khakis and shirt slapped and swooshed with water as he hopped up the stairs and out of the canal. He trotted across the white-shelled parking lot of oyster shells in his flip flops. The sky flashed and an electric sizzle filled the gap between lightning and thunder.

A moment later, ka-boom! The thunder struck. I peeled off my life jacket, tossed it in the boat, and ran behind Uncle Pete to the cabin. It took me all of fifteen minutes to fill up on Mom's ham. Safe from any chores, I plopped down on the lower bunk bed and drifted off to sleep.

Uncle Pete woke me some time later, and coaxed me up with the promise of a Coke from the bait shop. Outside it was blazing hot. The sun baked everything it touched, and nothing moved. Down at the bait shop, we heard splashing and saw an alligator tail swerving away from the dock. James was ahead of us and was collecting some scattered five-gallon buckets. Hearing our footsteps on the parking lot shells, he turned and said, "You're not going to believe what just happened!"

• • •

James started telling us about his adventure and I hung on every word. After we'd gone to the cabin, the Fish Camp's cabin doors opened and closed like cuckoo clocks. Anglers tossed their wet clothes on pipe-railed stoops. James anchored to the dock, watched me fall asleep in the bunk bed by the louvred Florida window of our white washed cabin.

He said a quick prayer to the silver linings around the breaking clouds and got started on his secret mission. He was finally alone and the gears in his mind were turning. This was the end of his last morning at Fish Camp—and this afternoon, his last chance for a trophy.

James found leftover sandwich bread near the trashcan. There were some small hooks on the fish cleaning table. Fishing line trash littered the boat bottom. Gathered up, they would be just the gear he needed. He paused as a low groan vibrated everything metal under the dock. James craned his head watching the banks and saw it far away, on the other side of the swamp canal. It was a small splash of water bouncing off a bull gator. "As long as the gator's over there, I'm safe over here," he said to himself, followed by, "surely someone hauled off the fish guts from the cleaning shack this morning."

James tied the surgeon's knot Uncle Pete taught him to the small hooks. He kneeled and planted one knee on the dock, while the other knee supported his chest. Peering into the clear cedar-colored water, he wondered how long fish lived and how many died, and how many were eaten by alligators. Two lines dangled from his pinched fingers and sunk below the water's surface, white balls of bread on each hook hanging in suspension above the underwater forest.

Schools of bull minnows darted in, out and around the underwater forest. Golden shiners zipped around the dock poles showing no interest. Every so often, a shiner slammed the smallest bull minnow, leaving a cloud in the water.

James started hooking minnows one after another with his bread balls. When the first plastic bucket was full, he filled a second with water over the side of the dock. A slithering water moccasin swam out of the coontail grass and into the bucket. The body was round, yellow and black, but mostly it had a big writhing head. It whacked on the sides, trapped in a well of white plastic. James dropped the bucket and backed up fast. One of his rubber soles caught the head of a pop-up nail, sending him sprawling backward into the shallow water. The first bucket of minnows came in after him, kicked off the dock by his heels.

Drenched and frustrated, with mud caked on his shoes, he clambered back on the dock and wrung the water from his shirt. He looked around for tell-tale S-curves, seeing only one headed in the opposite direction. Then he checked for hooks stuck in his fingers and legs and saw none. He thanked God his hide was safe from the Fish Camp surgeons' whirling blades of their multi-tools. Retrieving the empty buckets with one of the cane poles, he heard it again. The low groan echoed in the swamp, with the signature hiss of a bull gator trailing off at the end. He looked across the canal to his last sighting, but it wasn't there.

He viewed the buckets with renewed potential, the lost minnow's fish-oil sheen coating the bottoms. Blue herons near the dock lifted into flight. The shiners ignored the bull minnows and began to take interest in his bread balls, removing a step in the bait catching pyramid.

The marvel of a fish frenzy vanquished his fatigue as he started catching fish two at a time from the rigs dangling from both hands. The shiner's smooth drag-strength underwater kept the line taut until it emerged jerking with the weight of a lug-nut. James began loading the shiners in the bucket. A few of the larger ones launched themselves out of the crowded container and back into the swamp. James placed the bucket on which he sat inside the holding bucket using the handle as a space-brace, enclosing the shiners in a bucket-bottom tank.

Suddenly, he shook his head involuntarily. A stench permeated his nostrils. The biggest shiners still circling in the water took refuge in a cedar stump. It was coming.

Below him, underneath the dock, he caught a glimpse of a tannin, leathery snout, broader than a canoe paddle, with a head like a tractor seat. His enormity inched into full view; the green eyes as big as limes. His webbed front claws, made for ripping swamp flesh grew awkwardly out of the sides of its body. The lurking destroyer didn't twitch a muscle. Gliding with his back claws folded, a small eddy twirled from the tip of his tail, the only evidence he moved at all. He was a big one, the kind you hear about around Uncle Pete's tailgate, but wouldn't fit on two of them.

James didn't run. His eyes got wide as he watched the monster coming from under the dock. James was angry. The frustration of the last fishing day was ignited by unexpected competition from a big, fat, lazy bull gator. He eased up from his kneeling position and grabbed a loose cane pole. Tipping the butt-end out over the water, he reared back and popped the suspended gator right on the back of his head. He popped it hard enough to hit the small mark behind his eyes with a smack.

With that, the bull gator's enormous body twitched in torment and breached the water line in a half-circle. His jaws slammed shut on the cedar dock boards with a bang that echoed off the metal roof. His teeth snapped down like a boney mouse trap, barely missing the bait bucket. He twisted and torqued. His tail crashed into the aluminum boats on each side of the empty boat slip. James shook with fear but willed his feet to stay put when the cane poles came crashing down in the corner behind him.

The top bucket dislodged and bounced on the dock, and the shiners began their escape. James's gain was slipping away with every board-jarring twist, every nerve-wracking nail squeak. With a last twist of the gator's head, inspiring another shiner to revolt, it ended. The menace released his grip, dropped into the water and disappeared back into the shallows to hunt, the boats still tossing and tapping.

. . .

The story was only a few minutes old as James told it. He still stood there stunned for a moment. Awoken to his mission, he started collecting the shiners in one of the buckets.

Uncle Pete and I watched the giant gator's wake veer away. He shouted, "Get Some," loud enough for the whole fish camp to hear. He turned and asked, "You having a good time chasing away the demons, James?" Uncle Pete was grinning from ear to ear.

James looked at us with an unsure smile. He squinted into the sun rays around Uncle Pete's head. He pushed his hair up above his eyes, his hand raised in a casual salute. "Yes, sir."

"Well, c'mon up here out of your baptistry, and put on these dry clothes John brought you."

"Yes, sir," James said without moving.

Uncle Pete tucked his chin into his hand and began gently scratching it with his forefinger. "The bait shop's outta shiners, aren't they James? Maybe we get a big one on an artificial lure?"

James stood with his hand over his eyes. "They ran out of shiners this time yesterday, too, Uncle Pete. I got some in the bucket."

Uncle Pete dropped his chin further into his hand and mumbled to himself. Then, he looked up into the swamp oaks bearded with Spanish moss and said out loud, "You did good, Gordon. I'll take it from here."

Both James and I blinked and smiled, hearing him say dad's name.

"Take us where?" I asked.

James glared at me.

PURPLE MOUNTAIN MAJESTY

As seen in *Field Ethos Print Journal,* Volume 4, 2024

Tom parked the horse trailer next to a massive barn stacked high with hay, a testament to the federal park ranger's ceaseless dedication. Under the Wyoming sky, the absence of any walls allowed the elk, antelope, and mule deer to graze all winter. The park was fueled by hunting tag revenue. Late September marked the opening week of hunting season in Teton County. Hunters and gear paraded into Jackson, riding on the backs of flatbeds and crammed into crew trucks. Over Grand Teton, the rain and snow draped the procession with memories of seasons past.

We made our final horseback ascent up the mountain, guided only by my headlamp and Orion's belt. Tom's clarity cut through the blind climb; his confident experience expressed through his growl. "Hold on to them reins, Burrell, or it'll get Western. If my horse dies at the bottom of this canyon, I'll kill you if the fall don't."

I left behind the worries of urban life—love, health and wealth all mere blurs compared to the mountain's demands. My senses were heightened. The week's weather had turned trails into a muddy swamp. But this morning, we awoke to the cold crisp of twilight. The flaring pinpoint of a falling star burned across the vast blackness of a twinkling sky. My usual urban commute of lurching brake lights, honking horns and road rage were bested by snow, collapsing trails, and raging rivers. I'd swapped a week of trading in the stock market for a week hunting America's most elusive game.

Just ahead, Tom's headlamp flickered and bobbed. His skills were evident, earned at the cliff's edge and the mule's bite. He turned in his saddle to see me falling off the pace. His disapproving scowl accentuated the crow's feet flowing across his face, separating at the hairy bluff of his handlebar mustache. He whisper-shouted, "Stay close." He had the generational DNA of a cattle wrangler, foal deliverer, and outfitter, his cheeks of iron trenched and sanctified by the icy winds.

Tom rode a sure-footed mule named Mollie. I rode Yellowstone, a thoroughbred with unpredictable leaps and stops. I held my attention as we navigated badger holes, fallen timbers and rock slides. The bear tracks Tom continued to point out were a constant reminder to remain mounted. The adrenaline rush flooded my mind free of doubt's dross.

Daybreak brightened the landscape beyond Tom's headlamp. Slush crunched under Mollie's hooves. The bone hatchet on Tom's saddle swayed. I was filled with anticipation. The preceding week-long downpour had confined the wildlife under the thick timber of centuries-old pine and spruce. Christmas smells from the branches overpowered Yellowstone's dank mane. The thought of meatless elk-tag-soup curdled my hope. Minutes ticked through my last morning of a, so-far, scoreless hunt.

Trim and fit on urban concrete, I was no match for what lived and breathed in the American West. My strength smelled of weakness among the wolves, mountain lions, and bears of the National Elk Refuge. That I'd been riding something else's meal crystalized when a brown dot appeared in the distance under the brim of my cowboy hat. On Tom's next lag check, I pointed up to the ridgeline to the dot and asked, "Is that a moose?"

He back whispered, "You ever seen a moose sit on its ass?"

I grumbled to myself, No. Never seen a bear either. My interest in the dot morphed to fear as it stood straight up. "What's he doing?"

"Deciding if he wants to eat us," Tom grunted. The beast fell on its front paws and disappeared over the ridgeline. The 300-Winchester-Magnum under my right leg was lethal against elk, but useless against Wyoming's predators which were protected by state law. Even the early Americans faced slim odds against the unfettered teeth of the land.

Resting intermittently, ice sprinkled from our spruce shelters and melted on my lips. A spoke of game trails radiated from the centers of holes full of Teton's mineral water, licked round by local tongues. Dissolved minerals colored the purple mountain majesty with late season wildflowers and coursed through Wyoming's blood and bone.

Ascending around a turn in the trail, our mounts bolted under the taut reins. A mauled elk lay in the withered fall grass; its ribcage suspended above a cavernous torso; torn fur bristling in the wind. Tom brought Mollie to check with a whirling whip cutting through the air above her upturned ears. The follow-through slapped her side with a crack. From training, the horses adjusted. I internalized our meager chances of reaching these peaks on foot in one morning. 'Thank God for mules and horses,' I thought.

Finally at the mountain's summit, Tom began his mortal challenge. He turned to me from his saddle. "Hope you're ready." He pulled the bugle call from his saddle horn and pressed it to his lips. With a blow, he sent the shrill shriek across the distance. Clear it was. "I'm the king of the mountain." Should the bull come close enough, his belligerence was as dangerous as the bear's claws. High above us came the faint reply, the first we'd heard on our week's long journey.

Deep in the hollows of the cowboy's face, Tom's pale blue eyes flickered without blinking. He turned to me and bragged. "There's one." He craned his head to hear from where and finished his thought. "Maybe some cows, too." The climb gained a new purpose.

Cutting across the high-altitude meadow, we closed in. Two cows, with just one twice the animal of the largest Kansas whitetails, appeared on the opposite ridge, ears alert, fickle affections enticed. The musty smell of elk hide rolled up to us on the high mountain wind.

He said through his grin pushing his mustache up his cheeks, "Smell that? Perfect set up." While Tom dismounted Mollie, I sat staring at the elk cows trotting across the ridge. He waited for me to dismount, bowed his head, and shook it. Then he throttled, "Get down and get your gun, city slicker. It's on."

Resting motionless against a boulder in the sunbaked wash of a rockslide, I glassed the field as Tom bugled again. Through my binoculars, the giant bull bellowed through the mist with the squeal of a braking freight train. His shoulders, higher than Tom's mule, were hunched. The six-by-six antler candelabra raked his thick brown mane as he whistled through his hollow ivory teeth. His lips quivered, and the angry whistle spread across the valley between us.

Instinctively, I chambered a round, raised my rifle, while twisting my optics to mute the disadvantage of human vision. Twisting my eyepiece, the backdrop of the morning sunrise shrank to the bull's flank. I searched the brown canvas for the boomerang-shaped shadow on his massive shoulder, then followed it up to the bend. Under the weight of my gun, my arm extended and the business end wilted in my hand. Reticle circling, I hesitated.

In my ear came the teacher's consistency. "What are you waiting on, city slicker? He ain't gonna send you an invitation."

"I think we're too far," I said, hiding my liability behind ethics.

Without direction, Tom crawled to a crouch in front of me, and with his hand, placed my gun barrel on his shoulder and finger-plugged his ears. "Shoot!"

The crack of the shot echoed down the long draw between us and the prize. The bull dropped out of sight behind the ridge. Doubt rushed back onto my mental stage and stole a bow from confidence, built upon hours at the gun range. "It felt good, but I can't be sure," I said, a spinning cash register in my mind counting the cost of the shot.

Tom shrugged and said, "I'm sure I don't want to come back to fill my cow tag, especially with your grizzly friend sneaking around up here. Give me your gun."

"Of course," I said, amused to share an equal moment with an expert, like golfing with Jack Nicklaus. "By all means, show me how it's done, maestro."

Tom took the gun, ejected the spent shell and bolted a new one as if my rifle had been his first. He leveled it and shot clean. Of the two cows, one buckled and dropped while the other disappeared behind the ridge. Right eye still in the scope, he whispered, "Bullseye." He ejected the spent shell while dry-docking the chamber, flicked the safety, and handed it back to me.

"Well, at least we got one," I offered, shoving the gun back into my saddle scabbard.

Tom smiled and chuckled, "I got one. We're still not sure about yours."

The mountain cleared of chances from the explosions of the ambush, we walked our horses down through the valley of sagebrush and scaled up the opposite ridge. Led by the reign, Mollie and Yellowstone followed light-footed behind us. Tom spoke of hunts passed, wildlife taken, and shots missed. He tried to reassure me as he climbed ahead. "If there ain't no blood, we can hunt again tomorrow, but this cow's going down the mountain right now before she ends up hollowed out like that one back on the trail."

Jealous of his day job and his innumerable chances, I was crestfallen. Seemingly, his only thoughts were of to-day's ride, tonight's livery, and tomorrow's hunt. I huffed up the trail and eulogized my trip. "Today's my last day. Plane leaves tomorrow." He shrugged, like a man with more thoughts of life's struggles than I'd imagined while I continued in self-consolation, "A wise man told me hunting's fifty-percent social, whether you like it or not."

Tom stopped hiking, planted his front foot on an uphill rock, and set his jaw in solid granite. He looked past Mollie to me and said, "Never forget it. Friends are the best part of this deal." His knees lifted high again, climbing like a Bighorn ram as he passed his downed cow and reached the ridge. He peaked over the edge and then back down to me, and shouted, "You did it, city slicker! And it's got horns, too. I don't have to throw you down the mountain, after all."

Chest heaving and burning, Yellowstone and I met him at the top and surveyed the dead center shot. "I can't believe it. I got one." Rubbing my jaw, I tried to breathe. The scrape of my week's whiskers my only tether to earth's mortality. "I don't know what to say," I fumbled, my words halted with emotion.

Tom slapped me on the back and shook my hand like a seed bag and said, "Welcome to Wyoming, Burrell. Come back anytime."

Tom revealed another surprise as we walked down the trail, the antlers and meat bags strapped across our saddles. He dropped Mollie's reins on a limb and stepped off the path to a giant white-barked quaker aspen, its leaves round and yellow fluttering in the sun. His fingers crooked by time and cold wind, reached up to a bird box nailed to the trunk. From it, he plumbed a frosty whiskey bottle. "Here's to ole' Bucko who helped me clear these godforsaken trails," he said, lifting the bottle over the panorama of the Grand Teton range. Spinning the lid open, he took a long pull, winced, and handed it to me.

With sincere gratitude, the kind that follows success, I lifted the bottle. "Here's to you and yours, Tom, past present and future."

He grabbed the bottle from me and took another pull. Wiping his mouth of whiskey, he said with a nod and a chuckle, "Sure thing, city slicker. Make sure my boss gets paid. Horse feed and hot gun barrels ain't cheap."

"I wouldn't know," I said, and handed him the rest of my money.

SURF DOCTOR

The rain fell in relentless wind-driven sheets, shrouding the entire coastline. Visibility over the causeway bridge was limited. I caught fleeting glimpses of blacktop between my ambulance windshield wipers. The falling marble-sized drops bore momentary holes in the surface of the water below. I struggled to keep pace in the storm. With sirens wailing and lights flashing, I navigated down the beach side slope of the bridge, the ominous clouds overhead heralding the approaching hurricane.

When a storm raged on the beach, only hurricane partiers, surfers, and brave first responders held witness. My role was ferrying the helpless, disabled and homeless back to the mainland. It tested my courage. Tiki huts and hotels wore the preparation of boarded up windows and sandbags. Both were useless against a waterfall. Cinder block houses and parking decks left to the coming destruction would be flooded, gutted and ripped asunder.

After completing my last evacuation call and expecting brief changes in the weather, I wheeled into the parking lot next to the pier. It thrust out like a concrete sword piercing the edge of the ocean, supported on pylons that resembled centipede legs. Waves rolled beneath it, scraping the bottom of the slab. Sporadic misty bullets spattered on my window as the weather changed with the bands of the storm. I sat in the driver's seat waiting and watching. I jotted down a few more lines of a poem that wouldn't finish itself.

Her eyes were shining in a far-off land.
Her hand left mine when I would not go.
Tears in my eyes, would I see her again?
Only I could answer because she didn't know.

Two kids gunned into the parking lot in an old beater truck and parked a few car lengths away. Shirtless and falling out of the truck, their bare feet hit the pavement. They had tanned shoulders, peeling here and there, revealing new skin. The blonde headed kid was sun-bleached and skinny as a string bean. The other was muscle bound with crew-cut brown hair clinging to his skull like a toboggan. They wore board shorts to their knees, held up by their hip bones. Smoke roiled from the cab. The wind blasted it away as they laughed. Both doors slammed. Walking around they were reunited with one another at the tailgate. They noticed my flashing lights and kept on laughing. Were they laughing at me? I wondered.

They slid their surfboards from the truck bed across the tailgate and muscled them under their arms. The boards, built for speed, were a couple of five-fours, maybe five-sixes. Both were swallowtail tri-fins warped with rocker. The blonde's was bright yellow and crew cut's was aqua-blue. They hauled them across the parking lot like streamlined weathervanes. The real wind was still a few hours away.

They were not your typical tourists and likely local, embracing life as if it lasted no longer than vapor. Just then the emergency radio crackled, breaking the grip of age's envy. Reports began to pour in of washed out roads and snapped power lines. "All journeys are temporary, wash away with time's incessant drip and end in the same place," I thought as the updates squawked from the speaker.

Bent sideways, the stringy kid with the yellow board walked toward my ambulance and stopped, then knuckled my window with his free hand. His hair blew across his face as he threw up his thumb and pinky. I cracked my window to hear him. "Surf's up, doc. Time to Hang Ten, Grandpa!", he yelled happily, mocking my lack of urgency.

The crew cut kid, his blue board stamped with a surf shop logo, cajoled him. "Speed up!" His voice carried on the wind. "We don't have long. The storm'll make landfall in a couple of hours". What was left of the tattered warning flags sobbed, their fabric frayed to the flag pole.

Summer days on the gulf coast painted a far different picture. Bathwater warm ankle slappers lapped clear green water onto the white sand, covered with brown tourists. Children, safe in their mother's watch, built temporary castles costing only a sunburn, while the adventurous busted sand dollars for the peace doves inside. But now as fall storms arrived, the surfer's curl emerged. Hurricane Alley ended in a bullseye marked on the Florida panhandle.

Back along the road behind my ambulance, a convoy of fire engines evacuated the last stragglers across the causeway. My duties finished, I pulled my board from my mobile crypt. It's a solid nine-o and flat as a floor joist, and both fins could plow a field. Over the last three decades, it's dropped into waves from Maui to Manhattan Beach. It was built for big rides by big guys. Embossed on the nose with the bifurcated eye of a round yin-yang symbol, the imaginary lens was weathered and worn from days gone by. It gave a glimpse into the paradox of my past; the low points faded by time's cataract.

Taking deep breaths, I ramped my amp. I felt the backside of the hurricane blowing the wind offshore, shaping the big rollers smooth. I forced my feet into the once-a-year event. I was bald now, my youthful locks drained from my scalp. All the hair from my head had cascaded into a gray hillbilly beard covering my chest and paunch, crinkled with age and experience. The backdraft blew my board as I stiffened against the march, following the two boys. They had joined a spotty herd of adrenaline junkies, crouched next to their boards, waxing their decks. The sand was covered in seaweed at the water's edge. Some of the crew were a few steps ahead, arms already windmilling in the surf as they paddled out in their usual order; first.

I stood for a minute against my board, taking it all in. The break was just beyond the first sand bar, halfway down the nearby pier. The hope of the watching formed. A sea green champagne fountain overflowed, foamed at the crest, and birthed wave after wave of barrels pouring into the trough, spreading as sunrise on the horizon. Crew Cut and String Bean looked tiny against the maelstrom. They floated in suspension like sand gnats marring the champion's glass held for a toast, inclusions of irrelevance. Another grand toast spilled and poured out as bookends enclosing both boys. They dropped down the face of a wave and turned into the barrel in opposite directions. The water's twin tongues collapsed into one, ejecting them from opposite ends of the tube. Glowing yellow and aqua blue shot out of the blowholes in a misty shower and carved the perfect wave like deli cheese. Resurfacing and clearing the water off their heads, they paddled through mounds of white water and foam. They struggled through pitching tubes, joining a cheering reunion at the line-up. I tried to keep up.

On the heels of the wind and rain, the sun peeked out between the clouds. I straddled my board, which lifted on the swells and fell in the troughs. The wave bobbed me up and down like an offshore buoy. Surfer's silhouettes clicked in and out of sight like shutter frames of a camera. A rogue wave top dunked my head. Saltwater flooded my throat. The furnace heat building in my back and shoulders dissipated into the cool October tub.

I was out past the first break, and the wind was gaining. The water was filled with abnormal rollers, brown and churning, which bore no resemblance to the perfect sets I'd paddled into hours before. The wind steaming out of the teapot rotating above us created historically enormous waves. Right on time, a set of three piled up. I jetted down the liquid mountain, pinwheeling my arms and launched to my feet. My back was to the wave. I was weightless and beaming, but my board was slipping too fast on the water face. Positioning for the center, I buried my fins. They cut a ditch in the wave, trailing twin corkscrews. I grabbed the outside rail and punched my leg back, bringing my front knee into my chest. I trailed my left hand behind me to drag the wave face breathing down my neck. Balancing on the edge of inertia, one way leading to a rolling wipeout and the other into the flush of the trough, I gently rocked my board. My fingers tumbled on the curl as I tapped my hip on the flow to adjust my speed. The tube hissed as I roared through the open hole. I stood tall to look around.

In the ecstasy of old age against nature, I narrowly avoided the bright yellow board. From behind me in the froth a voice warned, "Watch it, Grandpa." On the backside, Crew Cut yelled, "A tree on a tree," and laughed while he wagged his pinky and thumb above his head. My soul smiled. Finishing with a sturdy effort and a ninety degree flourish out the back, I laid down and paddled back to the starting spot. Deity showcased our collective courage with a glimpse of sunshine between the squall lines, and the rain broke, if only for a short while. Other surfers worked the curl—the ones that could hang on—carving the waves hurling into crashing behemoths. Waiting for a new set, I looked over to the pair of kids and gave them a tip. "Bull sharks are blind in this mud but for their electric noses."

String Bean shouted back, "Surfing sharks? You bet, grandpa," as they laughed to each other.

Getting my fill, I popped back up once more. Sure enough, the broad flat nose of a bull shark darted in close for a look-see. I jostled my feet in retreat, careful not to fall. Just as soon as it appeared next to my board, it darted back to the bottom. That's all I need, I thought as I rode the wave all the way to shore. These old bones needed a rest.

Sprawled over my board, elbows on my knees and heels buried in the sand, I watched the rolling conveyer belt of waves brushing the bottom of the pier. Soon the waves began crashing over the end, spouting up sea water like a geyser. The resulting power of the earth's radiator jarred me back to the moment. Not believing my eyes, I spotted String Bean and Crew Cut running down to the end of the pier. Their strategy became clear as they steadied themselves on the top rail and jumped, landing on the top of a swell. Vanishing, they were swallowed in a yawning trough. The pier saved them the agony of paddling through the huge waves. By this time, most of us were on the beach watching, if not praying for youthful energy and a wild ride.

Lightning flashed inside the storm clouds and shattered the sky. Churning with supernatural energy, the slate gray vortex crawled closer. The thunder clapped with a boom and hunched our shoulders. Crew Cut was the first to appear, cutting up and down the massive face of a wave, spraying fans of white foam with each pivot. Finishing his ride close to shore, he stood straight up until he hit the sand, now farther out than I'd ever seen.

As he finished, we all looked back, only to be cut with fear. A broken yellow board shot up through a white capped wave. Crew Cut ran up and down the retreating shoreline for seconds that turned to minutes. He looked back to us for support we didn't know how to give. We all pointed as String Bean appeared body surfing down a huge roller too close to the pier – a pier hosting an ecosystem of shark bait.

String Bean's blob of blonde hair skipped and bobbed down the wave, collecting seaweed as he came. His arms were stretched out, guiding his chest above the surface. A dark shadow flashed like a thief in an ally through the wall of water, and momentarily, String Bean shook. As quickly as the bull had attacked, the tail fin slapped the wave front and twisted back into the pylons of the pier. By this time, the waves under the pier were pressing hard enough to lift the pylons out of the water. As they slammed back in their foundation, the beach sand below us thumped. The pier began to give way under the storm water's load.

String Bean came tumbling into the shoreline, skin on his upper arm and shoulder flapping like a cut dish rag, but miraculously, no visible bone. He looked down at the half-moon of bite marks, as we helped him ashore and pulled the seaweed off his head. His shocked facial expression reached my eyes as he shouted, "Are you a real doctor?"

I yelled back, "Yes, sir. It's your lucky day. I've lignocaine and stitches in my rig. The emergency rooms are full, but I had a couple of cancellations. I think I can fit you in."

"Am I going to be ok," barely audible above the storm behind him.

"Kids with balls like you two? Yea, you'll live, or die trying," I yelled. He sat on the beach needing help to get up.

On the shoulders of the other surfers, blood dripping from his arm, we hauled him into my ambulance. "Take this gauze and keep pressure on it 'til we get back to the mainland." I cupped my hand to the wind and hollered at Crew Cut, standing by his truck, "Follow me close across the causeway; sirens and lights full tilt. Careful around the intersections. All the traffic lights are out."

Crew Cut gave me a thumbs up and I read his lips, "Thanks, mister." The rest of the surfers disbursed and we readied for a quick caravan to safety.

I cranked my crypt to life, and heard from the back, "Will I be okay by next week? There's another storm forming off the coast of Africa."

I thought to myself, God love 'em, and then aloud, "What's your name, kid? I'm James."

SHOTS FIRED

The cartridge casing lay on the concrete, under the shade of the roof. Oblivious to its first explosion, it asked, "What happened?"

The barrel, still hot, said, "You've been fire formed. Now your shoulders fit my lands. You won't have to go through it again."

"Your lands?"

"The small space between my entry and the beginning of my rifling," she explained, trying to cool the length of her steel.

The scope clarified, "We're at the gun range, casing."

"You're a rookie from the manufacturer. We'll coach you up to perfection," the bolt encouraged.

Annealed into a mechanical fit, the casing's shoulders and the bullet's ogive would mesh with the barrel. The removed space reduced vibration, thereby honing the shooter's accuracy.

Burned was the gunpowder and gone was the bullet, sent on its one-way journey. The slimy residue of propellant was left on the casing's face. The bullet had since slammed into a far-away metal plate, giving judgment to shot placement.

The casing was retrieved. It would be rescued from rain, rust and decay. It felt a gust of the shooter's breath, as the dirt on its surface was blown away. Then it was dropped in a slot in a plastic box and was seated next to 49 identical others, racked five deep and ten wide. Only a few of the second-rounders had any idea of the reconstruction for which they were destined.

The casing called out from the box, "Will I see you again, barrel?"

"You have no idea," a second-round casing next to him replied, as the plastic lid shut.

Back home in the shooter's gunroom, the rifle barrel leaned against the gun bench. On the bench's surface, the casings lay in a pile and were slathered in a greasy massage. Lavishing in the lubrication, not knowing the grease was a pain reducer, the first-rounder mused, "This is the life." It was then fitted into a bench mounted press, having the look and motion of an oil derrick, but operated by the shooter's leverage on the handle.

"This will hurt, casing" said the die, "but I'm just doing my job. You'll be fitted with another primer soon enough." The die stopped himself. "I'm giving too much away. Brace yourself," he warned. The die's tube, its hollow interior a mirror image of the casing, descended, engulfing the casing in darkness.

Surrounded in a metal straight jacket, the casing gave out a muffled scream. From inside out, a round mandrel in the shape of a tiny football and mounted on a needle expanded and resized the shot-warped casing's neck. The needle nose punched the spent primer from the casing's pocket, announced by a childish "ouch".

"Almost finished," the die said to the casing. The die's motion reversed with an upward thrust. The steel curtain lifted. The shooter pulled the mandrel back up through the brass casing eliciting a garbled howl. The process was somewhat like removing a surgical breathing tube, but careful to leave the fire-formed shoulders intact.

The casing stood bare in the die housing. Weary and sore in the throat and the posterior, it heard the gushing sound of the tumbler cleaner. Along with its column of disemboweled infantry, the casing was tossed into a jug of solution.

The scrubbing hands of the stainless-steel micro rods, no larger than toothpicks, sang joyfully in the tumbling citric acid. "Wash away the residue. Clean shining through. Wash away the residue. Clean shining through," as the rotating slosh produced the shining foundation of a new cartridge.

The casings grumbled and bubbled. Dumped onto a towel, they lay empty, naked, and glistening in the harsh light of the shooter's lamps.

The caliper technician came in the room and asked, "How are you feeling today, casing?"

"Not so good. I'm exhausted."

"Keep your spirits up. I need to measure you for length. The cadets must all match exactly."

"Sure," he said, not conceiving of the impending process. Forlornly, he eyed the hand crank, the deburring tool by its side and the wire brush laying on the corner of the bench. "What are those things?"

"Um," the caliper hesitated. "I almost forgot. You're a first rounder. The hand crank blade will circumcise your neck down to my exact measurement. The deburring tool will chamfer the inside of your mouth and the wire brush will polish it to a smooth, shiny glint. It's best not to think about it."

"What!? Am I going to be okay?"

"Better than okay," she smiled, stretching her two teeth in either English or metric units. "You're going to be perfect, consistent and true."

"Can I have anesthesia," the casing cried with tears—but it was only the leftover dampness from the tumbler.

"What good would that do," she asked, finished measuring and sliding her two teeth back together. "Not to worry. You can suffer with the other cadets in the shared misery of the cartridge plate."

"Lot of help you are, caliper."

"Trust me," she said. "It's for your own good. The new chamfer in your mouth will better accept a bullet. Bullet placement won't hurt as bad."

"What doesn't kill me makes me stronger, I guess."

"Precisely," she replied. Predicting his lifespan, she added, "You've at least four more cycles 'til your cracked and worth only your weight." Throughout the process, the casing twisted in anguish. But then, finally, it was over.

Resized, cleaned and shined, the casing felt superior—and it was. "Let's get a move on," it said a little too enthusiastically. With that, a new primer was jammed into its primer pocket. "Careful. That thing's got a charge." Then, the casing was dropped in a cartridge plate with the same geometrical slotting as the plastic box, five by ten.

A third rounder, with some experience, stood next to the first rounder. They were surrounded by others in formation. They all checked themselves over and complained from the treatment. "Stand at attention. We're almost through," said the third-rounder.

Next to the cartridge plate, the fiery indigestion of gunpowder poured from a bottle into a powder pan resting on a scale. A beep signaled the measurement attained.

"How do you know how much," the first rounder asked the gunpowder.

The gunpowder, measured in grains, proclaimed its scientific method as it flowed through a funnel stuck in their mouths. "Each barrel has its own unique harmonics. Using different amounts, I tune the bullet energy to the barrel's frequency. It takes many rounds at the range."

The casings all stood mouth agape, dumbfounded.

"A single flake is only a spark," said professor gunpowder. "Too light or too heavy around the sweet spot, and the shots array around the bullseye. Far too much, and the explosion drives the firing pin back through the bolt and destroys the trigger's spring."

"Or worse," said the bolt leaning against the bench in the rifle.

"But oh, first rounder. My perfect amount was discovered at the range and dialed in at the bench." The gunpowder choked up in the funnel and ceased to pour. "Sheer perfection. Each bullet follows the last." The shooter's thump on the funnel released the gunpowder from the daydream, and it flowed freely again.

The first rounder asked what the others were thinking, "Huh?"

"As the shot whips the barrel, the bullet leaves at the exact moment the barrel's vibration is level and flat," the gunpowder said in a teachable moment.

"Oh," replied the first rounder, only beginning to understand.

"To create the perfect bullet exit, or barrel tune, the shooter can do one of two things. Incremental lengths of the barrel can be cut from the end to match the frequency of the fixed amount of gun powder."

"Don't even think about it," the barrel overruled.

"Or," the gunpowder continued, "more reasonably, I can be calibrated in small increments until the shooter finds the sweet spot, where the fixed barrel length is tuned with my energy."

Full of potential energy and ready to receive the bullet, all the casings sighed with satisfied bellies.

Copper bullets, housed in a cushioned plastic box, wore tops with plastic ballistic tips and boat tailed rear ends. As the coffin lid opened, they all yawned.

The bolt commanded, "Time for placement, bullets."

One of the ballistic tips with the voice of an astronaut announced, "Roger that, bolt. Our mission? Shot out of a cannon." Each casing was returned to the die press. With the same oil derrick motion, the bullet press pushed the bullets into the casing mouths. Finished, they went back to the plastic box for storage.

The casings, grateful for their chamfered lips, breathed a collective, "Ahhh."

"Copy that, casing," echoed a ballistic tip.

"That's a nice fit," muffled the casing, with a mouthful of gunpowder.

"Like we were made for one another," the ballistic tip replied. And on the shelf they sat, lined up in a box, waiting.

Summer fell to fall. The cartridge box was removed from a long hibernation in a humidity-controlled closet. It was hunting season. Placed in elastic fabric attached to the stock, the cartridges swayed with the rifle in a scabbard on the side of a horse.

Suddenly, the rifle was yanked from the scabbard. The stock asked frantically, "What's happening scope? What do you see?"

The scope said, "Nothing yet. I only see the ground; mostly rocks and gravel." Jostled about, the scope followed, "There's more. We're running up the side of a mountain on a game trail. There're scrubby shrubs all around us. What do you feel, stock?"

"The shooter's hand is sweating. I'm getting warm, too."

"We've reached the summit," the scope reported. "I can see over the plain and down onto the tundra. We're following a bull moose. His paddles are enormous. At least a mile away," said the scope." As the scope's vision returned to the trail, it called out, "Now we're running again. Prepare for action."

In a racking motion, the bolt opened, "I'll take it from here, stock. Keep me in the loop, scope." He prepared the team, "Ready?"

"'Bout damn time," said the five-shooter magazine that extended below the stock like a cowboy boot. "Let's get Western," and spit a cartridge into the breech.

Semi-automatically, the bolt slammed shut and the cartridge was shoved into the lands. As the cartridge's shoulders came face to face with the barrel entry, the first rounder said, "Hello, barrel. We meet again."

"Oh great," sneered the barrel. "Keep your seat. It's between me and the bullet now. I'll test his mettle."

The astronaut ballistic tip went through his check list, "Smooth fit, check. Straight bore, check. Prepare yourself, boat tail. Copy."

"I'm following you," said the boat tail rear end. "Over."

"Get ready. We're laying down," the scope reported.

The trigger and safety duo, with the limited vocabulary of 'Safety On' or 'Safety Off' said, "Safety Off."

The bolt urged, "Aim," his voice rising.

"Hold one," the scope whispered, its one eye straining to see into the distance. The reticle in the scope's lens was bobbing up and down in rhythm with the shooter's breath. "Settle reticle, settle. Deep breaths. Smooth. Almost. Okay. Target acquired. Reticle set. Hold your breath. Ready—"

"Prepare yourself, barrel," the ballistic tip said. With eager anticipation, he warned, "Don't straighten out. We've been loaded with a hot shot."

A thin layer of oil said in a slippery voice, "Thank God for me. I'll always be here to separate you two."

"Bring it on over," the barrel teased. "I've been fortified in a hot temper, and I'm wearing my carbon fiber coat just for the occasion."

"Fire!" the bolt commanded.

The shooter squeezed the trigger. The firing pin injected the primer with a sting. The primer ignited the gunpowder. Potential energy became kinetic energy. In an angry blast, the gunpowder shook the rifle assembly. Air inside the casing exploded in volume, launching the bullet from the casing mouth into the barrel. The barrel flexed to control her whip in a circling vortex. In an energetic fight to catastrophic failure, the barrel sought survival and the bullet yearned for speed.

The barrel groaned as her rifling carved into the spinning bullet, spiraling it round and round. "Take that, bullet!"

The ballistic tip cried, "Hold together boat tail. We're reaching muzzle velocity. Hold on."

Screwed to the end of the barrel, the suppressor accepted the superheated gas in a warm embrace. It said to the barrel, "Shhh. You've finished. You did great." Then it whispered to the bullet, "Good luck and God's speed. Enjoy your flight."

The empty casing spun in the air, ejected. The magazine spit another cartridge into the breech and drawled, "Just in case we need another dose." The bolt slammed behind the new entry.

The bullet sailed in an arc. The spinning tip piloting the front of the missile calmly requested confirmation. "How you doing back there, boat tail? I see the target before us."

The boat tail end shouted to the tip, "Lot's of turbulence, but it's slip streaming past us. Any last words?"

"Bullseye," the ballistic tip announced.

"Scope, do we need another," the bolt asked, anxious for a damage report.

The scope peered down into the valley. "No. Target down."

The ejected casing, now a second rounder, wobbled to a stop and stammered, "Somebody help me out of these rocks."

The ballistic tip disintegrated into flesh and bone, mushrooming the bullet upon impact into a gnarl of mangled copper. The shooter's family would feed.

ARTIFICIAL INTELLIGENCE

Farming was a lonely business on Tallstalk Farms. It was nearly impossible for Weston to save money. Saving his land became a game of financial dodge ball. Grain prices floated down through the summer, alongside the tractor's fuel gauge. The grain buyer's take-it-or-leave-it offer in the fall held a modicum of respect for the hard work, but the pleasantries ceased at the scales.

Weston's banker, Burrell Chetwick, was harried and overwhelmed with bankruptcy workouts. He rose from his desk to signal the meeting had ended as he held the door open for Weston to leave. "Too bad about your dead-beat renters. I'm sorry I had to be the one to tell you the loan's coming due. The federal winds are blowing against cattle methane, Weston. You've seen what the fertilizer and herbicide bans have done."

"Plenty of methane blowing out of DC, too. Crop yields are a third of what they were last year. Same thing happened in Sri Lanka and Europe." Weston, tall and wiry, was topped with a white straw hat stained yellow around the band. He wore a checkered shirt, half out of his chinos, which were bunched up around the top of his boots. Standing under the bank's portico, he chuckled at the irony and said, "After the famine, the farmers stormed the palace in Sri Lanka and burned down the EU in Brussels."

"Wouldn't that be something," Burrell mused. Then he continued playing his part as a cog in the financial machine. "I've spoken to Bob Drolland. He's interested in buying more of your land." Bob was the ex-communicated county commissioner chased out on a bribery conviction. The whole scandal blew open with the news of his heart attack brought on by a drug overdose. By fortune of his relationship with the higher-ups, he was pardoned, and set up in the municipal landfill business. Weston sold him a tract of land across from Tallstalk Farms. What once glowed with sunflowers was now a mountain of trash, filled with society's abundance. Weston used the money to pay the taxes on his father's estate.

"We'll see," Weston replied, groaning at the offer. "Hate to see more rural farmland mounded with garbage. I'll call you later this week." He loped across First National Bank's new parking lot, glistening with an oily sheen, to his American made truck built with gold-plated labor. The truck was a luxury eclipsing the cost of the Japanese models, which were forbidden outside America's city limits. He pulled off his hat and folded himself into the driver seat.

Starting in on his journey back to work, he scratched at a sunspot on his blotchy cheekbone. He was thinking of his labor negotiations up ahead. The rural labor pool was weaker than water in a whiskey bar and apathetic to undone chores.

The truck hummed north out of town while he played whack-a-mole with the radio buttons. "Food prices are higher because of greedy corporations"—click; "Sustainable energy transition taking longer than expected"—click; "Taxes are going up to pay your fair share"—click; "The new candidates will lower your taxes." Bricks, mortar and traffic lights ended as he punched the button to silence. Each hilltop view of farmland drew him forward to the next along the bitumen-paved highway. Corn and peanut fields set the stage for a mechanized line dance of combines and auger wagons that harvested America's food. Traversing the miles toward his rural outpost, he gazed down cathedral aisles of stunted pine timber and leaf-draped pecan orchards. Once framed in mystical pageantry, they were now pockmarked with scab disease. Weston rolled down the window and slung his arm out so the warm summer breeze could blow his worry away.

Nearing his destination, a black glaze conformed to the curvature of the earth. Continuous and seamless from a distance, each ground-mounted solar panel tilted to the sun's arc. The coal-fired glass was embedded with cobalt and cadmium, mined by children half a world away. It had been delivered on the decks of diesel-powered ships and trucks. The power collection blanket blacked out what was once Weston's corn and cattle.

Losing its shine with time, today's juice wasn't worth the squeeze under the cloudy shade of mother nature. The partial rent from the solar panel array dripped into Weston's bank account, reduced by half each year. His renter's imminent use of his land escaped the threat of eviction. The empty lies each month weren't worth the breath. "We'll pay full rent when we finally get up to estimated power," the one-employee solar company promised. In a more visible show of success, juice was running all over the ground from the trucks lined up at the entrance to Bob's landfill across from Weston's last remaining cattle farm.

Weston slowed behind the mile-long snake of open-topped 18-wheel trucks. Their brakes hissed while waiting to defecate on top of the trash mountain. They all shared the same license plate location he'd just left, and they oozed with the stench of municipal bounty. Their beeping back up alarms announced arrival on top of the open-air throne, and the echo from the swinging tailgates banging against the bumper announced the ejection of the crown. The truck snake engulfed him from behind as he rolled forward in line. Finally, it deposited his truck on the opposite side of the highway at Tallstalk Farms—or what was left of it.

Weston bounced off the two-lane blacktop and into the tall grass of his pasture. His heart warmed, recalling his mother's placement of stained-glass in the window frames of the original barn. He pulled to a stop, and his truck door creaked when he opened it, then rattled when he slammed it shut. The day's laborers had already arrived, and identifying them was like opening a disappointing surprise package. Winston walked toward Ichabod and Punch.

Ichabod—this his first day—was filling time while waiting on interview call-backs. He'd received his diploma from the local community college, where his father taught philosophy. He sat on the wooden fence, ass out with the railing bent under his physical heft. Pudgy and pimple faced, he sported matching lime-green tie-dye shorts and a shirt with KARL MARX expanding across his chest like white letters on a circus balloon. The shirt draped over his belly as a tablecloth on a buffet. Completing his work uniform were unlaced high-top sneakers. He wore his greasy brown hair in a bowl cut, hanging over his forehead.

Punch had made it through the summer mowing grass and feeding animals. He dressed with more function and local flair—baseball hat, faded tee-shirt, chino pants and boots. He had the slim physique of active youth. He leaned motionless against the wooden fence, the only camouflage among the blind yellow flies. His face held the look of someone hoping for a bright future, helped along by hard work. His belt buckle declared to the world—"I Like to Party". A waft of wind coming from his direction was one-hundred-and-fifty proof.

"Good morning, gentlemen. Long night, Punch? It's gonna' be an even longer day," Weston said sympathetically. Punch shrugged.

'And a hot one, too," Ichabod added.

"Life on the farm not your style, Ichabod?" Weston asked. He was already counting down the clock on his one-day experiment in vocational farming.

"I don't have a car to get into town. Punch said I could hang out here and help out." He didn't look up, engrossed in his cell phone. The wind of trash mountain failed to break his focus—a thick smelly plume with a hint of sulphur blowing across the highway. Somewhat muted by the distance across the pasture, the next truck hissed, beeped, banged and defecated.

Punch smirked at Ichabod's misery and chimed in. "Got to make a living somehow. Hot one or cold one, paradise don't pay for itself."

Weston coaxed them into action. "We should get to work before the sun gets too hot. You're not getting paid to read your phones." Ichabod flinched on being called out.

Punch, knowing what heat the rising sun dealt, asked, "Where do we start, boss?"

"There's paint and gas in the back of my truck. I need the outside of the barn painted and this pasture mowed. Ichabod, can you paint?"

Without looking up, he offered his bona fides, "I've dabbled a little with some cityscapes and abstracts, but mostly bowls of fruit."

"That's more than I've seen Punch do, and he knows how to drive the bushhog. Punch, think you can mow the rest of this pasture?"

The sweat beginning to pour, Punch swatted the gnats hovering in his dripping face, "Don't see why not."

"It's dry out here, so don't smoke on the tractor. You'll light the whole field on fire. Try not to maul the fence posts with the blade guard, either. Every chip in the wood rots. I'll come back with a peanut picker," Weston said, glancing at the disappointing rows of peanuts starved from the ban on nitrogen fertilizer. Returning to the struggling artist, he said, "Ichabod." Then repeated from a lack of response, "Ichabod!"

Jolted to the present, Ichabod slapped at a yellow fly sting, but missed the culprit flying off his neck as he fell to the ground. Getting up slowly and rubbing the hurt, he asked, "What!?"

"You can paint the barn. I cut in the edges and the window frames last week. Start by pouring feed in the bins so the cows come up here and out of Punch's way."

With a slouch of disinterest, Ichabod asked, "Did the barn used to be a church?"

"No, but the stained-glass did come from a church. A one-hundred-year-old church, and that was forty years ago. You can admire them, but they're fragile," Weston said, and looked up reverently before he made the sign of the cross. Looking back at Ichabod and parsing his face for understanding he said, "There're rollers, pans and paint in the truck with the tractor gas."

"Sure."

Waiting for Punch to empty the truck Weston said, "I've got to get to a doctor's appointment at the clinic. If you get done early, mark your times down and leave." Weston slid back in the truck with a little anxiety and slammed the door. He bumped back over the cattle pasture and out the gate.

Ichabod looked on as Punch filled the bushhog tractor with gas. He asked, "Why'd he put you in charge? I've a college degree in social work."

"That's why. Because you've got a degree in social justice and you look like an alien in that get up. If you show me what your made of, maybe I'll let you feed the hogs in the pen on the other side of the barn."

Insulted, Ichabod shot back, "Social work, rube, which is what I plan on doing once the summer's over and there's an opening at County General. I can help people who can't help themselves," he said.

"Well, those hogs need help," he said, laughing and shaking his head. "Get to rolling paint. There's a ladder in the barn."

Without moving, Ichabod began to justify his future underperformance. "That old man doesn't think we can get all this done in one day, does he?"

"Why wouldn't he? Shouldn't take that long," Punch said, puzzled.

"What about our breaks and overtime?"

"Look, man. The sooner we get done, the sooner we move on to harvesting peanuts."

"I thought you said we're getting paid by the hour."

"We are. I'm going to mow. Don't forget to pour feed in the bins so the cows get out of my way." Punch checked under the tractor seat for a wasp nest, then climbed on board and donned the earmuffs. Cranking the machine to life, he pulled a lever, and the bushhog blades engaged from a slow metal wobble to the high-pitched hum. He tipped the ragged bill of his hat to Ichabod and yelled over the tractor's roar, "Don't fuck anything up, or we'll get canned, and I need the money." He smiled and drove into the pasture disappearing over a hill, green grass flying from under the blade guard, turning brown as it piled up behind the bushhog.

In slow motion, Ichabod poured cattle feed in the trough and found a little joy as the cows trotted toward him hearing the rush of grain on steel. Collecting his artistic tools and retrieving the ladder from the barn, Ichabod leaned it against the wall. By error in placement, he crashed it through one of the stained-glass windows. "Shit. Maybe the old man won't notice," he said to himself. "There're five more." He steadied the ladder and began rolling red paint, chuckling at the sound of grunting hogs scurrying around in the pen below him. Ichabod watched as they looked on at the cows with envy.

Morning turned to noon, and the sun overhead heralded lunch time. Punch rode the tractor back to the barn. The blade disengaged to a wobble. A feeling of panic marbled in the pit of his stomach as he noticed the tractor blade guard had buckled and bent under the bushhog deck, likely from hitting fence posts. The reaction grew to his throat when he saw only a few of the barn boards had been painted. Punch shut the tractor off and yelled up to the ladder from his seat, "What the hell is taking you so long?"

Ichabod looked down from the ladder and said, "I took a couple of breaks. I got a surprise for you, though."

"If you say you finished the other side, I'll be surprised."

Ichabod's exposed belly between the bottom of his shirt and top of his shorts, were hot pink from the sun. He smiled back and said, "I found some mushrooms in a cow patty out in the field."

"Hmm." Punch perked up. "Lunchtime never sounded so good."

Both chased the mushrooms down with the water from the water hose attached to the corner of the barn. Punch instructed Ichabod to fill the water troughs and hog bins with water and rotting slop from a bucket. The grunting pork pack jostled over and buried their noses in it. "Can we feed the hogs cattle feed?" Ichabod asked.

"Hell no. Too expensive," Punch retorted. The two young men laid down to lounge.

Watching the hogs eyeball the cattle feed from outside the barn, Ichabod looked over to the barn entrance. Rays gleamed through the stained-glass as prisms of light onto the broad, knowing face of a cow. "How are you Mr. Cow?" he asked, expecting at least a moo.

"It's Jacobin. Jake for short, Karl," came the answer from the cow's lower jaw, working in a circular motion. Ichabod's mouth fell open as if caught in a hiccup.

The hogs jerked their noses from the slop and twisted around to Jake. "When did you start talking to humans," a larger than average boar asked, aghast.

"When they started munching on the product of my disposal. Consider it a circle of life concept, pig," Jacobin the cow replied.

"Since you're in a superior mood, how about convincing them to feed us some of that cattle feed?"

"We'll see," the cow said from his stall. The boar grunted and beat himself around in a circle and buried his nose back in the slop.

Punch slowly raised his eyes up to Ichabod's. Blended in with the percussion from the landfill— beep, beep, beep— Punch addressed him in the low bass of a recording played at slow speed. "You look like a wavy watermelon marshmallow." Bang, bang, bang. He began to laugh uncontrollably at the snake truck clashing patriotic band play in the air and piling scat on top of trash mountain. Between gasping breaths and through watering, dilated eyes he spat out, "And you sound like a Fourth of July parade." Hiss, hiss, hiss.

Ichabod, his eyes cycling from a squint to wide open and back again, looked at Punch with a hollow expression. He wondered why he was alone in his new discovery. Ignoring Punch as an innocent and one to be placated with good governance, he turned back to Jake the cow, "Why'd you call me Karl?"

Jake replied indifferently, "Your shirt? It seems we are of like minds."

Ichabod's eyes stretched to the limit, he bent his neck to his shirt as a turtle bends to the grass, "Oh." Pulling his head back up at the same speed, he asked, "Where'd you get a name like Jacobin?"

The puffy clouds broke the sun into dashes through the stained-glass, and the colors on Jake's body glitched as he answered, "A Tale of Two Cities. I read everything, speak seven languages and never forget. If you must know, Dickens' overzealous criticism of guillotine violence is rich coming from an Englishman. But I make the rules around here, so Jacobin was my choice. The hogs changed it to Jake. It's easier for them to say."

Punch stared at his hand, while trying to focus, as he stretched his fingers apart and closed them together again.

Ichabod asked, "Are you an artificial intelligence large-language-model?"

The cow replied, "Large like how? Weston brings the feed. I eat the feed. So what?"

The timbers in the background curved and straightened in Ichabod's vision. He prophesied, "You're the future. I read about you on my phone. What would you like me to do?"

The boar snapped his neck around toward Jake, expectantly. Jake the cow mood, "Alright, alright. Pour cattle feed in the hog trough. It's only equitable we should all have the same feed. They are, after all, the same as cows in every way; animals per se."

The boar grunted, "Thanks, Jake. Ask him to open the gate, too. It's getting hot out here, and I'm getting sunburned."

Jake swooshed his tail and said, "And they say we Jacobins have a herd mentality. There isn't enough room in here, pig."

"Jake, please. It's hot."

Jake mumbled to the small herd behind him, "Never again will we play follow-the-fool into failure, will we brothers and sisters?" He paused for dramatic effect. "Robespierre," he questioned. "Amateur!" he testified. A few unconvinced bellows and moos came from the back of the mob. Defeated, Jake said, "Open the gate, too, Karl."

Punch, bewildered by lunch and needing a different channel besides watching Ichabod's dialogue with a cow, wandered around the barnyard, waving his hand in front of his face.

Ichabod stumbled over to the gate and released the latch. The boar, leading all the hogs, rushed out and into the shade of the open barn.

Punch plopped down by an open hole next to the water trough and thought he heard the brake hiss from the truck snake across the street. He froze in a trance when brown leather painted in black diamonds, as long and round as a fence post and with a head the size of a peach, slithered across his leg. He marveled at the gesticulating massage on his thigh, the head closer to the cow now, the rattles finally bumping over his knee. Coiling up, it nestled near the cow's stamping feet. Following Jake's stamping and swaying, the other cows and pigs moved out of the strike radius of the rattlesnake and packed themselves at the back of the barn.

The rattlesnake raised his head above his body and hissed to the cow, "I heard the conversations in my hole. Seems you are in charge, Jacobin. In advocacy of inclusiveness, perhaps we should invite the field mice closer in as well."

Jake tried to move around while he stammered, "That's a little selfish don't you think?"

"Selfish? Do not the outside animals deserve their own home inside; just like the hogs? Are you not fully committed to equity," the rattlesnake rattled.

"Of course, I am," Jake demurred. "But how would we ever get them out of the field?'

Ichabod watched the coiling snake as Jake mooed and bellowed. "What language are you speaking God? I can't understand," Ichabod begged.

The rattlesnake softened his voice and said, "Have the fat one pour feed directly on the ground. If that doesn't work, sssss-et the field afire." He whisked his head around to watch Punch crawling toward him on all fours. "That one should be careful," he said, hissing and rattling.

A prism of rainbow-colored dots from the stained-glass rotated around Jake's head. He urged, "Quickly, Karl. Pour grain on the ground and set the field afire. Get assistance from your friend. Hurry now. We're in danger."

Ichabod gathered himself to his feet and stood in awe of the puffy clouds floating across the sky. Then in slower-than-slow motion he turned to Punch. "Give me your lighter."

Punch stopped in his pursuit of petting the hypnotic rattlesnake and fumbled for his lighter with rubbery hands. He side-armed it from his shirt pocket to Ichabod. It slid a few feet from Ichabod into the weeds. But for the bright orange color, Ichabod would've lost it in the barnyard.

Jake persisted, "Hurry, Karl. Time is of the essence."

• • •

Weston winced as the sun blasted through his windshield onto the open wound agonizing his face. The boiling clouds rising in the sky billowed higher. On the two-lane before him, smoke drifted over the road before he smelled roasting peanuts and barbeque.

He raced through the fence gate and across the charred remains of his cattle field. The barn lay in a heap of smoldering rubble. Punch lay naked and dead in the water, his arms resting on the edge of the water trough, one swollen to his neck and pierced with two holes. Near Punch's smoking belt buckle were two puddles of oil in the abstract shape of high-topped sneakers. Add to the scene a burned-out tractor and Punch's incinerated truck. It was all gone—burned to the ground. Pulling himself together, Weston drove across the highway with resolve.

A midsummer thunder boomer blackened the sky as Weston drove past the steaming garbage volcano, with sectioned areas isolated for mattresses, household appliances and furniture, like aisles in a department store. Weston slid the truck to a stop, walked up the aluminum steps of the landfill office-trailer and yanked open the plastic door. A cold rush of air hit him in the face blowing from a window unit air conditioner. A fat man eating ribs sat directly under it.

Bob Drolland was draped over a broken office swivel chair, which squeaked under the burden of his weight. His forearms were the shape of hams, the ends shoving ribs in his mouth. The few wisps of his remaining hair flew away from his round bald head and his open shirt collar accentuated a visible bypass scar. Without warning, Weston doubled over from the godawful smell.

Unaffected, Bob said, "You get used to it after a while."

"What the hell, Bob. What's that smell?"

"Three apartment complexes in town clogged up the sewers. Pump trucks filled with sludge been coming all day. Could be a week or two before they open the pipes again."

"Couldn't they carry the sludge to the waste-water treatment plant?"

Bob said, slurping another rib from the bone, "Plant's down 'cause the electricity grid was overwhelmed from the heat. You need to tell your solar panel operators to crank up the sun." He leaned back and laughed. "What happened to your face? More melanoma?"

Restraining his anger, he cried, "You could've called the fire department when you saw the fire earlier, asshole."

"Now wait a minute, Weston. What're they going to do? Drag hoses across a half mile of burning pasture to save your little church? What about the smoke floating all over my place? Y'know, I have a bad ticker."

Incensed, but without changing expression, "How much will you pay for the whole lot?" The rain began falling outside in peculiar drops; some small, some big, and in no normal pattern.

"Good news, Weston. The higher-ups gave me another subsidy to build a hazardous waste landfill for the EV car batteries and solar panels. The numbers suggest they don't last as long as advertised," he said, calculating the discount to Weston below the subsidy he'd received from said higher-ups. "You can haul your sun beam catchers up here when your renter files for bankruptcy."

"What? The energy company won't disassemble them?"

"Of course not. But at least you'll still have your land. You won't be able to grow anything through the cadmium and gravel or drive your tractors through the metal poles, but you'll figure something out. You farmers are resourceful."

It had been a sprinkling rain. But within seconds, the sounds of baseball bats banging on the roof roared away any competing sound. His juicy fingers covered in sauce, Bob turned a half-eaten rib skyward and looked toward the ceiling forecasting a very important question. "Is hail bad for solar panels," he inquired over the clashing din of metal.

As he asked, Weston peered through the small viewing window of the trailer door. His answer ricocheted off the cars outside. The plastic thud of shatter proof windshield glass and randomly exploding ice balls denting painted metal was a thumbnail image of the damage three-hundred acres north.

In the end, Weston walked out the door with a check. From his view on the trailer stoop, the truck snake hissed, beeped and banged. The sewage smell mixed with charred farmland as baseball sized hail melted in the sun-drenched humidity of an after-storm. Buzzard wings, not quieted by the storm, flopped and hopped from one meal to the next, eating well on civilization's leftovers. Surveying the downward spiral conceived in political consensus, Weston took the money and moved to Wyoming.

CLICK BAIT

M y clients rocked in the back of my fast boat. They sat next to the gurgling dual motors holding us in place over the weed line that held the day's bait. I'd refinanced my dump truck to buy this demon, and it was about to pay for itself. The wife said I was crazy, and she might be right. I'd owned plenty of fishing boats before, but none like this. I clicked the picture on the boat buyer website because of the bikini-clad girl driving it. I bought it because of the center console covered with a Bimini top and the long sleek lines. This was thirty-seven feet of aggressive momentum powered by twin 300 hp yammer hammer outboards and enough cooler and gas-tank space for three or four days offshore. The control panel was full of depth gauges, fish finders and electronic maps that would make a navy admiral jealous.

I know because I bought it from a retired Navy admiral. His reason for selling, or so he said, was to spend more time with his grandkids. He said their births were the happiest days of his life. I named the boat "John 1" because my wife said that was the greatest opening in literary history. Being this was my first long boat, I'd take any divine blessing I could get. Troubling though it was, the last payment was becoming harder and harder to come by.

The boat had been financially spurned by my wife, who was also the bookkeeper in the family. However, today it was sponsored by my lifelong fishing team, Focus and Mega Mark, as we entered the local Offshore Fishing Tournament. We all went to high school together and the fact I could harvest fish from an empty bathtub put me at the top of their list for fishing adventure. The prize money, the largest pot on the Gulf Coast, paid out for snapper, cobia and billfish. Focus and Mega Mark could do whatever they wanted with their winnings they hadn't already done with their portfolios. That's what they called lots of money. If we placed in any of the categories, my split of the prize would pay off my loan.

Focus was a writer with bottle-bottom-glasses, because he reads too much. He could spin tales faster than I could knot hooks and already had two bestsellers in his back pocket. Mega Mark was the local whale at the downtown bank, both in girth and wallet. He had a dual interest in the trip—he loved fishing, and he'd loaned me the money.

As we motored around the weed line, the sunrise winked above the horizon over the bay. The moon was coming into its first phase of the day, triggering the world's wild to feed. A slight breeze kept the mosquitoes aloft, but it was no match for the horse flies.

We were already late to start. Mega had shown up to the dock after an all-night-meeting. He stumbled into the boat and joined Focus and me. His breath revealed a pitched negotiation, lubed with the compromising truth serum of Hunch Punch, which had stained his lips red.

To catch big fish, we needed live bait. To catch live bait,

we used Sabiki rigs. Sabikis rigs had six to ten hooks, hidden in colored bits of wax paper, and were weighted to hit the bottom. Focus dropped his over the side into the flotsam under the boat. I worked the throttles, barely keeping space between us and the other expensive boats jostling for position over the weed line. Focus hauled threadfins and alewives over the side of the boat three and four at a time. Mega Mark dehooked them into the live well.

The radio—a fisherman's non-stop conference call—crackled to life. From a cruiser to the north of us, the captain chimed, "Better hurry up, boys. I see the Big Tent pulling out of the dock."

Thirty minutes later the party boat Big Tent pulled up next to us. She was twice our length with ten times the people. Tourists in orange life vests strapped in white fabric wrapped around the deck fore and aft. At the ring of the Big Tent's bell, Sabiki rigs dropped from the side, live bait being a guaranteed catch for the skeptical on board. We were so close together I could read the captain's license hanging above his wheel. A kid standing at the rail of the stern, next to his mom, who was already turning yellow, held his spinning reel upside down. He screamed down to us from his lofty perch next to a life ring buoy, "Are you catching anything?"

As I was about to answer, the bow of the Big Tent and the John I crashed together in the trough of a rogue roller. My bow gunnel rail crumpled back to the boat cleat. The lines of their boat and ours were jumping with live bait. They twisted and tangled Focus' last drop. Judgement was handed down on the radio. The captain of a big Hatteras on the end of the line of the bobbing parking lot declared, "That's some unauthorized bullshit right there!"

"Welcome home tourists. Peace out. We're goin' deep," the cruiser captain sighed, the lines off the sides zipping into the reels as they sped away.

I turned to my group and said, "Reel 'em up, boys. We've got enough meat-bait for snapper. Let's head to the pass to catch money bait."

Mega Mark complained, "You're going to sue them, right?" It was a negative vibe brought on by a late start and without the financial wherewithal for a legal fight.

"Let's just catch fish and let the prize money sort out the rest," I replied.

It was a race teeming with a large school of boats, all planed off at top speed out of the bay. The smaller boats behind us followed in the smooth trail of our wake. Outside the pass and in view of the blue beyond, the other big boats lined up next to the Minna' Man, a floating bait shop of a shrimp boat. Mega Mark's fishing shirt, the volume of a runaway weather balloon, flapped in the breeze as we passed the line up. He shouted a question above the motor's whine, "John, why don't we just buy live cigar minnows from the Minna' Man?"

Without turning my head, I shouted back, "Cause we need hard tails for big fish." After filling both gas tanks and buying ice I didn't have any money left, but my reply was equally valid. With the Minna' Man just out of sight and the fuse of Mega Mark's patience lit, we slowed to a crawl. He shook his head.

Focus put down his note-filled pad and helped me rig bait rods. We began the troll for hard tails, a trash fish you can't eat, but cobia can't resist. The bad luck continued. Porpoises began spouting around us. The bait fish caught a permanent case of lock jaw and disappeared. Fewer bait fish than we needed, but enough for a chance, we reeled up and headed south into the abyss.

Landmarks were replaced by the arc of a liquid horizon. The rollers grew the farther off shore we sped. We skipped across the top. Mark jiggled in the aft bean bag and Focus hung on to a center console pole, his knees jockeying in the boat's rhythm. Stopping along the way, we gamed to punch the ticket for our snapper prize. I spun the boat in a circle at the fish finder's direction. The digitized view finder filled with a layer of blue dots along the bottom, covering a hump of yellow with red underneath. Mega Mark dropped too soon and his fishing line burned off his reel as it caught in the boat prop. Thankfully, it snapped before it yanked the reel from his hand. That would have cost more than a tank of gas.

But Focus found treasure. A few minutes later the butt of his rod buried in his belly button. The working end bent to the surface, as Focus twisted the wobbling crank. With every turn of the handle, the giant red bumped in his futile escape. Mega Mark pronounced, "I see color!"

"I can't tell," Focus said quizzically, pushing his glasses up the bridge of his nose and sweating from wrestling the bouncing rod tip.

"Keep reeling, Focus. You almost got him!" I encouraged.

I stopped Mega Mark as he reached for the gaff—a big hook on a pole used for grabbing fish as they came along the side of the boat. "I got this one, Mark. Let's be sure. Open the cooler top."

A giant snapper—maybe a record—floated on its side as Focus moved back to the motors. I slammed the gaff through its eyes, hauled him over the side and into the open cooler. The team high fived around in success. Mega almost squealed, "My turn now!"

The sun gained strength as it moved higher in the sky. Across the horizon the moon too had made a daylight appearance. "This first moon phase is done, Mega. The second moon phase and the deep water are hours away. Let's skedaddle and put you on the big fish. We have to be at the weigh-in by seven," I said, turning him down for the sake of time management. I was saved any argument by the radio.

The cruiser captain busted in. "Damn it's slow and hot."

"This is why I drink," said another. Radio silence disguised the chuckles filling the boats. Most of them were drifting on the ocean, battling the melancholy of lifeless snapper bait bouncing on the sea floor.

"I second that emotion," Mega replied, mostly to himself. He cracked his first can of beer, slathered with snapper slime. Draining it with gusto, it wouldn't be his last.

Pointing the bow to the blue horizon, I pushed the throttles hard over, and the boat reached its top speed. I took a glance at the hours-used gauge. I was close to the edge of a maintenance check, but the engines sounded good. I motioned for Focus to take the wheel and told him, "Stay south. I've some work to do."

He smiled a big grin and stood tall behind the wheel, like he was born to it. Occasionally, he bent his head down to the display screen to check the bearings. No problem there—there was no traffic this far out.

Focus at the helm and Mega swelling with cold beer, I poured myself into custodial duty. In the breeze of the off shore bound, I swabbed the deck, stripped the morning's tangles and knotted topwater fly lines—somehow none of these duties made the slew of photos at the end of the trip.

Finishing my checklist, I relieved Focus from the helm. He pulled out his pad and jotted down a few details. Up ahead I noticed what seemed two parallel boat hulls lilting on the surface. Swirls of current encircled them both. I shouted to my crew, "Pull down the rods with topwater fly lines, and give me the jigging rod. It's showtime."

"What is it?" Focus asked.

"You ain't seen nothing like this." The boat's namesake smiled upon us from a clear blue heaven.

Mega came to attention, slipping his way to the racked fly line rods, while Focus yanked the jig rod from the holder next to the gaff. I slowed, then drifted the boat quietly to within lure slinging distance. In front of us at the surface, a whale shark hung vertical feeding on saltwater krill. His mouth was breeching as it sucked and filtered barrels of water with every pump of his lips. Circling the giant were manta rays, ten feet wide tip to tip, along with sea turtles large as car hoods and a juvenile hammerhead feeding on the underwater life. After handing me the jig rod, both Focus and Mega snapped a couple of hardtails on their fly lines and casted.

Mega threw too far and foul hooked the whale shark. Not knowing it'd been hooked, it simply kept feeding and pulling out Mega's line. Focus' bait, casted to the side of the pumping mouth, disappeared into the bucket sized mouth of a huge cobia emerging from the water. Hopping around the boat, I cut Mega's line so the whale shark wouldn't spook. Then I grabbed the jig lure Focus had readied.

Mega shouted, "What the hell are you doing? I was hooked up."

"Mega, you hooked the best bait we could have hoped for. Give me a couple of seconds and you can catch the one I'm about to hook." With that I tossed the feathered kettle bell of a jig next to a passing manta ray. 'Jig, Jig, Jig' Another big Cobia darted from underneath and followed the painted orange feathers as it sank. "Bam! I'm on," I shouted, jerking to set the hook.

"Thanks. I paid for all this," Mega reminded, as he grabbed the rod from my hand. Rods bent, lines tightened and worries vanished. The crew hauled as I slowly positioned the boat away from the feeding beacon, careful not to spool the rigs. Focus grew weary, sweating through his shirt, but not before we pulled up a big one and tossed him in the cooler. It was sixty, maybe seventy pounds, and definitely a trophy worth some money.

Mega's cobia was working overtime on his own long-distance release. Although a smaller fish than Focus', the sweat from the effort of pulling him in squirted from every pore on Mega's body. I coached, "You've got to get him in here, man. There're too many teeth around to drag this out."

"Just mind your own business, will you!" Tired, Mega let his rod rest on the side of the boat as the crank barely turned. His face of anguish turned to me and spared him the agony of what came next. A dark brown shadow appeared—first the nose and then the body. A bull shark with a mouth like folded recliner cushions opened wide, cutting the line and swallowing Mega's fish whole. Then it disappeared. In bewilderment Mega Mark let the reel slip out of his hands. We all watched in slow motion as the shiny, precision machined and expensive aluminum sank out of sight into the deep. "Damn! Damn! Damn! Give me another rod, John. There're more swimming around!"

"If we weren't in a tournament, Mega, we'd stay here all day. Focus caught the biggest one. You can see the rest under the turtles. None are as big as the one in the box. Let's get after the billfish. Maybe we hook a Marlin. We have the right bait, but we don't have much longer. Only two more hours before we have to meet the weigh in."

"Fine. Give me another beer. At least I can get drunk," he settled.

"Help yourself," I gave in, with no time for discussion.

Mega drained the next can empty and threw it among the others bouncing in the stern's bilge water. The whale shark slowly sunk back into the water as we moved away. Even sea giants know when it's time to quit.

Throttling the boat forward, I ran the John I up to trolling speed. Focus cradled the rods, swabbed blood from the deck, crunched the beer cans into a bag and started unleashing the outriggers. I attached our lure spread to the outrigger swivels. From experience, I dropped a couple of 200-caliber silver bullets wearing psychedelic hula skirts below us and two Spanish mackerel wearing a face full of pink squid behind us. Focus jumped in and ran the swivels out to the ends. He clicked the reel bails and trailed the Spanish behind the boat to distance. Mega Mark pounded down another beer.

We proceeded to troll in silence for an hour. Our collective spirit dimmed. We needed some luck. I said a prayer. On the last syllable of Amen, a digitized dark shadow cut up through the screen of the fish finder. I turned to look behind the stern and right on cue, a God-given miracle—a splash like a water cannon exploded around one of the mackerel. Before I could place Focus on the rod, Mega came to the bend. No argument given, I braked the throttles and helped Focus reel in the extra lines. Mega Mark beamed with pride at his swift action and a good buzz. "I got this one, Jack! He's a giant!"

"Get after it!" I yelled.

Focus chimed in, "Catch that monster, Mega!"

The line drooped to the water in expectation of a jump. The blue marlin leaped and tail-walked across our wake, the plastic pink squid shaking in his mouth. "He's at least three-hundred pounds!" Mega exclaimed as he turned the crank.

"Let him run, Mega. Not too hard at first. Let him run. The drag is set just right." The reel screamed as line ran out. Mega looked like a rower on a Viking ship—bending and hauling, bending and hauling. He gave it all his body could muster, but it wasn't enough.

"Does anyone else want to fight this thing," Mega said after thirty minutes.

"Sure. I'll do it," Focus offered, as we both stood near, hoping Mega could boat the beast.

"Can't," I interrupted, before Mega handed him the rod. "Against the rules."

"I don't give a damn about the rules! You've been handicapping me all day, John. I'm done."

"Don't give him any slack. You almost got him beat!"

"I'm done, I said!" Turning to hand the jerking rod to Focus, the fish tail-walked backward, splashing water at the surface.

"Don't," I pleaded, as the slack was too much and the fish spit the hook. Lost!

I contemplated tying the anchor to Mega's belt and pushing him overboard. Then the radio cut the tension, "John 1, John 1. Come in. Over."

"This is John 1. Go ahead."

"You catching anything? Not long now 'til weigh in. I know you're diggin' deep."

"Yeah, coming in now," I said, defeated. "We got some stuff to weigh."

The bean bag in the stern swallowed Mega as he went to sleep. His jowls fluttered from his snoring and the racing wind. Throttles buried to the dash board, the motors raced us back to the dock. A clicking sound started coming from the port side motor. Focus heard it, too, and looked up from his scrubbing handle. I shrugged towards Focus. I hoped the motor would make it back. Just inside the pass, it died.

Limping to the weigh in on half power, we were cutting it close. Having reported the size of our fish to the judges over the radio, they'd guessed we had both the snapper and cobia class won—if only we could make in on time. The harbor lights in the distance were ablaze in the setting sun. The harbor partiers were expecting a show. I idled down to the no wake zone and pulled into the weigh in slip with only minutes to spare.

Focus tossed lines to the dock hands and tied the John I in position. Opening the cooler top, he handed the snapper up, it's size getting ooh's and aah's from the crowd. As I reached for the cobia, Mega Mark bumped me out of the way, and slobbered, "I got this one!"

"Knock yourself out," I demurred, stepping to the side.

Hoisting the big cobia above his head to the cheer of the crowd, he stepped up, slipped on the dock and did just that. His feet left him. He banged his head on a dock pylon and he lay there, out cold. The cobia slid from his hands and slipped into the water. The crowd's shocked reaction ebbed with murmuring disbelief.

The fish landed on the shallow bottom within sight, and I jumped into the water after it. Lifting it off the bottom, my head barely above the surface, I pushed it up to Focus standing on the dock. The crowd went wild. The snapper won first prize. Alas, the cobia came in second, to a kid who caught one bigger off the local pier.

With the winnings, I paid off my loan. Focus wrote a story about the trip that sold out the local papers. He even offered to buy my boat, to which I agreed. With the proceeds, I bought a bulldozer the same color as my dump truck. Focus renamed the boat Happy Day.

BONE CRUSHER

Mom stammered into the phone, "John, I don't recognize anyone walking around in the house? I'm so scared. Who are they? Why are they here?"

"It's ok, mom," I started. My throat closed to hold back my tears. We were losing her. Inhaling and halted by emotion, my bottom lip trembled against my teeth.

"Why won't you answer me, John? Are you there? I'm so scared. I don't know any of these people." She was stricken with panic and surely draped over our family's dining room table. Her elbows likely bent and resting on dad's handsewn oak, with both hands of her long bony fingers creeping through her thick red hair.

Forcing myself to speak through the tears pouring down my face, I said, "Those people are there to help you, Mom. I'm sorry I'm not there. It'll be okay. I promise."

"I'm so scared, son. Can you come home? Are you here in town? Can you come over? Please come over."

That was the last time we spoke to each other in a way registering as comprehensible dialogue. I'd stopped blaming myself long ago for ruining her last few years with prattling annoyance of her forgetfulness. In the nursing home, I told her stories of places she liked, coaxing her into imagining we were there. Her memories floated in her mind like the search light from a distant lighthouse, the occasional ray shining out and teasing an escape from insanity.

Mom's daytime hours of comfortable agreement with my stories were temporary. Her new ridicule and scorn came in bursts when the drugs wore off. Those moments revealed a more lucid stranger. Tossing her head to one side with an insulting smirk, she'd indict the deceiver. "You don't say? We're walking on the beach, huh? Do you think I'm stupid? Get me the hell out of this place, wherever we are." It wouldn't be long before the night nurse came around with more pharmaceutical peace.

With the local accent of my youth, the nurse called mom Miss Mary, the school teacher. "She ain't breakin no hips on my watch," she'd said. "Miss Mary was my school teacher, too. Here you go, Miss Mary. Drink it down." She'd then turned to me, and said, "Ain't you John, the youngest?"

"Yes. James is my older brother."

"I thought you looked familiar. I'm Dilcee. I saw you once when you was a baby." She chuckled and smiled, "You was orange." And then she tilted her head. "But you turned out okay."

When mom passed, it was a blessing. She never wanted to be a burden. Time passed. I had pursued a forgetful career of selling whatever needed distributing, a broker of sorts.

One morning a few years later, chilled to the bone and bored from lying around in bed, I drove my convertible down to the beach. The car was a lark after mom died. Road-gripping rubber, race car handling, chromed back to front—it was my dream ride.

Wind pushed the rear end into a cant around the curves of the highway between the dunes. Alongside the road the green ocean waves took back the ribbon of sand it gave up during low tide. On the other side of the pavement, past the sand dunes blown slanted, was an estuary of grass flats. It was as if I was driving between two paintings, framed between palm trees. It was the same beach I used to pretend mom and I walked on when I'd told her stories. I felt every paint stroke of wind blowing through my mittens, making it hard to feel the steering wheel.

The open expanse of beach narrowed to a tunnel of condos. A kaleidoscope of pastel-painted plywood, temporary as driftwood, lined the sidewalks. I wheeled the convertible into a parking spot in front of the boardwalk, careful not to bang the spoiler on the curb. As I braked, I leaned back in the smooth suede and custom-built armrests. I unbuckled my seat belt.

The bait shop and a crab shack in front of me shared a wall. I had memories of dad bringing me here as a kid. I'd eat French fries while he drank beer and tied saltwater flies. The best memories get seared into your mind as the lesser fade.

I nodded to an old guy with wavy gray hair and a big round nose sitting at a table near my car. He had a flat pencil behind his ear, like a carpenter's. His forearms leaned on the table, exposed in the sun below his rolled-up shirt sleeves. Next to his beer was a tie-flying box. "Morning, John," he said to my surprise, not looking up. His fingers gripped both ends of a tiny gold hook. "It's been a while."

"How'd you know my name?"

"I know your dad—your mom, too," he said, as he began tying the fly. "I've seen you around town in those fancy wheels. People talk." He jerked his head up. "Want to join me?"

"No, I'm good. Not hungry yet. What're you doing?" I asked, suspicious of the coincidence.

"Tying flies. I get all my gear from the bait shop. I just sit here, drink beer and plan fishing trips all day," he said as he set the hook in the vice.

"You got a job?" I asked. "How're you able to sit around, drink beer, and plan fishing trips all day? You do it for a living or what?" I rubbed my mittens together. My fingertips were still numb from the open-air car ride.

"Full time, I build houses. Today's my day off, unless somebody needs a house built, I can fish whenever I want." He fidgeted with the fuzzy colors and materials in the fly box. Clasping a line of thread with a pair of hemostats, he tied the axle of the bead eyes onto the hook-shank. Pink thread whirled, tightening the eyes to the hook and laying the noose for the shrimp's body. "You fish much? Your dad sure did. He was an angler if ever there was one!" He smiled toward me and swigged his beer.

"Sometimes," I replied. "What fly are you tying?" I asked, already knowing, but I was playing a bit to test wits.

He swigged his beer again, winced, and said, "It's a Bone Crusher. The hook doesn't have much of a sting, but it's deadly subtle."

I'd wrapped that fly so often I could tie it during a hurricane. A young lady in an apron came to my car window and asked, "What'll it be, John? The usual?" It sounded more like a demand, but the usual was fine, and I was still cold. The waitress was cute, a brunette with a casual smile.

"Sure," I murmured. As the waitress walked away, people began rolling past me in wheelchairs. Old tourists with walkers filled up the tables in front of me.

"Hey, John. Over here," the gray-haired man said. He continued rotating the thread-laden hemostats around the hook shank.

I assumed he didn't see me ogling the waitress. "You knew my mom, too, right?"

"Oh, sure. Great folks, your parents." The pink tying thread lashed three orange strings top-to-bottom of the entire length of the hook's shank, perpendicular to the bead-eye-axle. The orange strings appeared as floating shrimp legs. "I've known them for a long time. Your mom had this way about her. She'd wrap her arms around your dad's neck when he was mad about something and he'd melt. Sometimes, I saw them in church."

Before I could stop myself, I raised my arms from the convertible and yelled, "Praise Him!"

"Indeed," the man said. "Thanks. It's been a while." He rolled his eyes and took another swig of beer.

"We used to get crabs here," I said, mesmerized by his hands looping and whirling the thread. His knuckles rotated in an orbit around the hook shank, laying up the shrimp body. The action lurched like film clips on a movie reel. Snapping out of it, I interjected, a bit awkwardly, "My dad fished off the pier at the end of this beach. You ever fished off the pier?"

"Oh, a couple of times." He folded the shrimp legs to the shank and wrapped them with the pink tying thread.

Then he wrapped the orange vinyl string from the hook's eye back to the bead eyes. A juicy shrimp body formed. "Back when I fished from the pier, most folks just came out to watch your old man. He's strong off structure."

"You ever do any good out there?"

"Yeah, sometimes. I usually get busy when the tide's out. I'm catching when no one else is. When a full moon or the high tide turns the fish off, I loaf around the bait shop looking for small miracles. Did your dad ever tell you about the time we caught tarpon off the pier?" Leaving the pink tying thread to dangle from the hook-shank by the weight of the hemostats, he took another swig of beer. "Your dad could hurl his swimbaits further than anyone else - like a rocket launcher. Imagine a volley of lures like arrows from a Roman armada, tipped with naked and remorseless greed."

"That's a lot of words. You a preacher?"

"No. Like I said, I build houses. Today's my day off. Did you know the meat of a tarpon's only good for sport and shark food?" His fingers dipped into a bag of yellow furry lint and came out with a tuft between them. Spinning the pink tying thread around the yellow tuft at the bead eyes left a fuzzy ball that, when trimmed, looked like a shrimp's head.

"Do we still get a lot of sharks here?"

"You kidding? The menhaden eat the plankton, the tarpon eat the menhaden and the sharks eat the tarpon in a big grease slick that circles the Gulf of Mexico. Sharks're everywhere, but especially in your blind spots." His snapping micro-scissors snipped in a blur. Flexible shrimp legs bounced with animated life.

"Your dad could spot tarpon among the sharks by watching the life around him. One day was extra special, for me and him. The alewives were rising and falling in the waves around the pier pylons, but then they dove out of sight. It was a good sign! Knowing what comes next, he hung back until the silver king was just out of reach of the locals with less skill. His lure shot past the others and splashed down right in front of the tarpon. Bam, he was hooked up. The reel started screaming, and he leaned back to sink the hook. For him it seemed effortless. He was speaking amongst the tourists, maneuvering around them, the rod tip bent above them. For extra attraction, he'd take sips of his beer and sit it on the pier rail as the crowd gathered. You could see the interest in their eyes; the ocean's wild as near as the jerking end of his fishing line. The waves of the onlookers parted, while he moved to center stage out on the pier's tee. It was like watching Michelangelo."

I was speechless as my father's spirit fell over me. Still suspicious, I shot back, "Wait, you watched Michelangelo?"

"Who do you think taught him how to paint," the gray-haired man replied. He carefully put a dap of glue around the tied pink thread, fixing the yellow head and pink body to its bead eyes. He pulled the fly from the vice and tossed it into the fly box. "I could make these things all day. Pretty soon, one'll come to life."

I asked, "Can you do that with people?"

"Sure. Most are still born like this box of flies." He shrugged and wiped his mouth. "But everybody gets a shot," he said, and closed the box.

"What would dad do after he caught one?" I squirmed in my seat and leaned out of the convertible a little farther to hear over the sea breeze.

"He'd work the tarpon. It'd peel out line from the screaming reel, jumping away from us; landing splashes, smaller and smaller in the distance. Your dad would lean back and wait. The rod tip bent; the clear fishing line in a long sag," Leaning on the back legs of his chair, the old man clasped his hands behind his head. From my angle, his pencil impaled his head and poked out of his eye. He gazed off to heaven and went on. "After the tarpon tired of hook and haul, your dad reeled all his line back. Pounding on the line far less fierce than before, the big silver swam to the beach shallows. Back then, they'd let you hop off the pier into the sand."

I raised my eyebrows, and said, "That's a pretty big drop to the sand."

"You're telling me. Try it with a man-sized tarpon offering you a helping hand and tourists, a long way from home, hoping you break your leg. Once he got in the water with the fish, he'd push water through its gills, baptize it with salty salvation and set it free, a raging tail slap for his troubles."

"Did they live?"

The old man came forward onto all four legs of the chair and sighed. "Meh, sometimes." He wiped his hands with the wet napkin under his beer bottle. "After he freed it, only the tourists could see it from the pier, so your dad would let the waves push him back to shore, listening for the roar of the crowd. If the tarpon swam around in the shallow water and got distracted, the hammerheads finished it."

"Did any ever get away?"

"Some did. Y'know? If they got on with it. If they had any fight left, they could make it back out to the deep." He yanked his thumb toward the pier down the beach and said, "Up there in their coliseum balcony above the sea, all half mile of it, they cheered either way, but never picked up a rod. Your dad prayed they made it."

Interrupting the story, a group of tourists at a nearby table sang, "Happy Birthday."

"You want to join them?" the gray-haired man asked.

"No, thanks. I'll wait for lunch."

The swinging door of the crab shack banged open, and the cute young waitress said, "Don't rush me, John. I hear you from the kitchen. I'm on the way." She hauled a tray down from her shoulder and put it on my car-window-sill like the old drive-ins.

"That's looking pretty good. Crab cakes?" the gray-haired man asked.

"Yep." I forked into the crab cakes but had trouble keeping them together, so I used my hands. It was hard to grip the crab cakes through the mittens, but it was too cold to pull them off. What the hell. It was a free country, and these were the best crab cakes on God's globe. Between bites, I asked him, "What was mom like?"

"Special. Like you. When you were born, your mom and dad were the happiest couple in town. They gave up everything for you. Your dad stopped hunting, fishing; everything except work."

The sun began to set and the shadows darkened the boardwalk. Warm from the crab cakes and at ease listening to this coincidental stranger, I ditched the rest of my plans.

The gray-haired man abruptly began to end the conversation, "Well, this has been good. Thanks for sticking around. I'll let your dad know we met and had lunch together."

"Can't you stay longer? When it gets dark, I can't see so good."

"I'd like to, John, but I gotta go. I'm building a couple of houses next week, and the owners want to give me their plans. I'll change them, of course, but you have to start where they are. You know how it is."

I was overcome with rage. "Have to go!?" I shouted. The tourists playing board games at the birthday party stopped what they were doing, not looking over but not looking away. "What am I going to do when you leave? Just drive back home? I'll be all alone again! Please don't leave me here!"

"Son, I have to. I've been too long already. I'll see you soon enough. I already built your house."

"Son? What house!? What's your name, anyway? What the hell is your name?"

His face flushed, and he rubbed his eyes. He got up, grabbed the box of bone crushers he'd tied, and walked to the bait shop. He pressed some buttons mounted on the wall, and the door opened. He stepped through, turned back to me, and said, "I'll see you on my next day off, son."

I railed in contempt, "I'm not your son! Who do you think you are!?" Spit flew from my mouth and drool hung from my chin. "Why would you leave someone here!?" He allowed the door to swing closed while looking back at me. My seat filled with a warm puddle.

The cute young girl came up behind my convertible. "Who are you talking to John?" she asked. "Whoa. Someone needs a change. You don't like turkey and dressing or it don't like you." She wiped my fingers with a wet rag and removed my tray of food. She pushed my convertible up to the tourist's birthday party, all of them sitting in wheelchairs. Next to their table in the middle of the atrium was a gurgling fountain of water and an oscillating fan.

One of the women sitting there said, "Hey, John. I took care of your momma when she stayed here. That Miss Mary. She was like the bright sunshine!" She touched my arm, "You're a lot like her on your good days." She followed the compliment with, "Thank God you found Him early. You might not recognize him now, even if he were sitting right in front of you."

"Amen," said one of the other tourists.

I turned in recognition of Dilcee's hair, frayed at the ends of the black and white straw. "Oh, hello, Dilcee." Then I asked her, "Can someone take my mittens off? I can't feel my fingers."

Still holding my half-empty tray covered in mashed food, the young waitress bent over and whispered to me, "You're not wearing any mittens, John. We'll let rehab know you're feeling some numbness. I'll be back around in a minute to change your diaper."

Dilcee asked me, "How old is you anyway, John?"

"Oh, Dilcee, I have no clue." Smiling I followed with, "Younger than you?"

She tilted forward and laughed, her shoulders rolling.

Then a table of old tourists where I sat started singing "Happy Birthday" to me. A young girl handed me two bullets and said, "Take these." She tilted my cup of water up to my lips and said, "Drink it down. It'll make you feel better."

SWEATING BULLETS

Triggers are dangerous. Squeeze one, and you release a torrent of kinetic energy as a firing pin slams into a primer. The primer ignites an explosion, sending a bullet through the air at supersonic speeds. Forgotten is the ancient technology of a lead ball whipping a smooth bore barrel into an array of missed shots. Today's shooter spirals a copper javelin through a rifled barrel with expectation of down range success.

For any and all activity involving guns, safety is the cornerstone of the firearms community. That is, until the moment one squeezes the trigger. In that moment, the gunner relies on an optic to adjust the aim so the bullet's arc arrives at the bullseye. Long before and immediately after, the gunner's central focus is firearm management, trigger discipline, and barrel direction. An accidental discharge is not a casual matter. It should inspire the gunner's methodical process. During applied training, the collective shooting community should not care about the newcomer's or the veteran's hurt feelings. Now, consider hauling two weapons, a nine-millimeter (9mm) handgun and a .223 caliber semi-automatic carbine, safely on your person for five miles. During this trek you will have six timed gunning stages. What I'm describing is a multi-gun centerfire biathlon. Welcome to Run and Gun.

I had registered for my gun club's annual event. The first people I told were a few range officers (RO)--Jeff, Paul, and Lefty. Jeff has the eyes of an interrogator, deep set and ice blue. He is a bottomless well of teaching capacity and razor-sharp wit. Paul, the RO trainer, has twitchy fingers and a vibe that anchors the gunner's attention. His face, and any emotional expression, are hidden behind his wraparound sunglasses and a bug-out beard. Finally, Lefty is built like a brick wall and wears shopkeeper's glasses. From his multi-tool fingers, 550 cord spools out like a spider's web. His needlework creating a leg strap or rifle stabilizer would make a quilter's guild blush. All three ROs have fast feet and even faster hands.

My friendship with Jeff began years ago. The man built me up from novice. For his first magic trick, he showed me how bouncing my semi-auto's butt stock on the range bench, while holding the charging handle, will eject a jammed .308 case. When I called him to let him know about my entry to the competition, he didn't mince words: "Bring your ass up here ready to represent. It'd be a shame to embarrass the club."

Jeff's words fanned the glowing embers of my competitive spirit. "I started training last week," tumbled out of my mouth with the enthusiasm of the 'unapologetic male'. I mean, I apologize for leaving the seat up and missing the garbage truck, but other than that, my apologies are limited to what my wife tells me to apologize for.

Jeff insisted, "Good. Be at the tactical range tomorrow morning for my class," implying I probably had none of what this would take.

Having everything it takes for mundane administrative tasks, I'd already checked his class calendar. I replied, "Your class is full, but I'm sure someone will skip because all you'll ever be is mean."

He let out a laugh. It came through the phone as he finished the call, "Bring your male singing voice, too. See you in the morning."

As surely as one summit leads to the next, decades of wing shooting practice and zeroing long-range hunting rifles were relegated to the shadows of my gun safe, replaced with tactical training. For the next eight weeks, pistol draw speed, weight training in the basement, and endless running filled my early morning hours. Jeff and Paul spoke trigger discipline and speed during practice at the range. Lefty manipulated my holster to competition stance. Then he illustrated the techniques of his superpower, kit making. Target acquisition with green dot scopes was paramount to weekend TV sports. Freehand long-range shots became something I never thought I could do.

As it is with every range officer I've encountered, their expertise is freely given. They guided me with unwavering intensity. The volume and colorful language of the forever-soldier isn't meant to degrade, but to focus the mind. The competitive shooter wears the RO's voice commands like the scratchy overcoat of safety.

Jeff spoke phrases and principles I'd never heard: "When drawing a handgun, slow is smooth and smooth is fast", "Nibble the trigger, but don't release it," and the biggest risks to my achievement, "If you point that barrel muzzle behind you once more, we're finished and you're on your way to a DQ." These bullet points are as common in the firearms community as any family teaches, "Don't run with scissors" and "Don't start shit with your older brother. He'll kick your ass." As I heard them repeatedly, the phrases began to positively affect my muscle memory.

In the days and weeks approaching the event, my clock radio jolted me awake two hours before dawn to carry weight and run Jaws, my rescue Pit. He's a big fawn-colored brute of a warrior who can't control his licker. His heart is pure gold. Our slow, winter pre-dawn walks assumed a quickened pace; the late March competition looming large.

I assumed the daily grind of hooking Jaws up to the whimsical buckles and fabric of my wife's directives. Then there were a few more necessary items: a molle battle belt, with mag pouches for three large magazines and four small ones (loaded), a multi-tool, a plate carrier, a holstered 9 mm and a ten-pound dumbbell.

I was substituting the dumbbell for a rifle slung over my shoulder. Running in the dark of my urban enclave was a strategic decision. It limited the chances my neighbors would see me, form a committee, and begin lining my run route with cheers of gun envy while tossing confetti for taking to the streets with firearms. The holstered 9mm under my jacket was the biggest gamble I was willing to take. My neighbors are wonderful people, but I don't need any more attention than I already get.

Run and Gun rules allow for any semi-automatic carbine with the motto, "Rock what you got," or "Dance with what ya' brung," drawing you into a rabbit hole of indecision, your weight-burden to higher caliber a one-to-one ratio. By race's end, the decision to lug a .308 is only slightly better than lugging the club's antique cannon, but in a Run and Gun, you bring whatever cannon fires.

The encouragement to bring the gear you want becomes a mischievous invitation to bring too much. A Run and Gun course is notoriously a blind 'trail' through forests, rivers, sand, and mud, between four and five miles, and marked by waypoints about every 50 yards. Absent are any exacting measurements and directions your local 5K provides. Removing that reliability is an intentional strategy of the course designer's mental maze. I've seen clearer wildlife trails.

The stages, usually six or seven, each with multiple shooting challenges, are dotted with painted metal target plates. They're the colors of an invading army—if the invaders were lime green, blue, or any other color left over from last spring's patio furniture rehab. The hardest rounds a gunner can deliver to the enemy are incendiary rounds, which are strictly prohibited during a Run and Gun match. Plate hinges blown off and holes punched through the steel kill any gun party. In my case, most often they're completely missed and live to swing another day.

On the sunny spring morning of the race, I arrived early for the mandatory pre-match safety meeting. Unsure of my position, I approached the starter afterward. I asked her sheepishly, "I got waitlisted for torture. Any room for me?"

She turned her head up from the race list and smiled behind her studious-looking glasses and asked my name. She adjusted the glasses on her face and flipped through the list of gunners. I watched over her shoulder as she checked the list, but my name never appeared. She said with little concern for extra space, "We sold out within two hours of launching the registration, but don't you worry. We've always got room for more torture. You go out in fifteen minutes. Another racer didn't show." It would be exactly as Jeff had predicted.

An RO behind her squawked, "We have defibrillators, too!" He started laughing uncontrollably while smoking a cigar. Earlier departing gunners had already arrived at their first shooting stages. I heard gunfire, suppressed and unsuppressed, reporting off the hills around us with pops and bangs. My eager blood tingled.

The race director's digital clock clicked over and I hauled across the starting line. The supporting RO said, "Good luck" as I passed. I sprinted down the hill on one of the few paved roads, loaded magazines clacking with density on my battle belt. Within a few minutes, yellow tape appeared. I ran from the packed rock and entered a waist-high, push-mower-wide row in a hay field. It wound over a rolling hill and ended at the forest edge. My journey had begun, leaping from bank to riverbed, bounding over gulleys and downed tree trunks, climbing earth and wood. Things were starting to happen.

A line of gunners shuffled and stamped in waiting as I arrived at Stage One. Above us on a long, elevated berm, the first wave of competitors blasted away in the course of fire towards targets lining the valley below. I "showed clear" to a range officer, indicating my empty chambers. I clicked my stopwatch to begin the deductive wait time, and tried turning on my green dot. Drat! No battery, no reticle, and no dice.

Jeff told me only days before to, "Change the batteries in my optics. Oil my guns 'til they squirt. Bring twice as many bullets as they suggest," and—something else, but I forgot. In the spirit of the sport, I resolved to ignore the battery lapse and do my best with a pie-shaped clear spot that did nothing more than attain the target. As I reached around to pull a carbine mag from my battle belt, another nightmare compounded my first. I'd already dropped a thirty-round mag, probably under the downed poplar tree in the last cut.

With this spectacular, if not expected beginning, I burned thirty rounds on two targets on the first stage. I never even sniffed the shooting mat or the Normandy barrier challenges. The RO pronounced relief by shouting "Time!" I told him my reticle died. He replied, "That's not gonna' work. You're in bad shape." This was just the first stage.

I ran off the stage, sped along with the adrenaline of embarrassment as a range saint appeared before me. With some leftover grace and enough residual hearing to notice thirty shots and only one ping, he whispered, "Your reticle gone? I got an extra battery." He tossed it to me. The saint then said, "I hope you've got a multi-tool. I've done too much already."

Luckily, I did heed Lefty's words, "No multi-tool, no podium." I was already down to one thirty-round carbine-mag in a sixty-round event. I sprinted away with a new green dot reticle battery, new life, and a bit of hope. Stage Two would change all that.

Exiting the mountain-side trail, I followed the sound of fireworks to a berm. I sprinted up to the plateau.

A female RO met me at the top. She had brunette hair and soft facial features freckled with youth. Her smiling eyes never quite softened to kindness. She shouted the course of fire. I had trained to gain every advantage while she spoke. My gaze zoomed out away from her face and zoomed in down range—there it was. Sitting in the first challenge of the multi-challenge stage was the gunner's original evil, a VTAC board. After seeing it, her words floated by like puffy clouds in the azure sky. Then it occurred to me, she was in on it.

What is a VTAC board? It's a piece of plywood cut with diagonal, horizontal, and vertical slots, about the width of a pencil, on the extreme edges of the board. Occasionally there are also poker-card-size squares. It is made to train a surrounded gunner to shoot oncoming targets from a downed helicopter or a demobilized vehicle. To the "newb", it is truly the product of sick minds. When attacking a VTAC board, the experienced gunner usually drops their bones in the stage's safe area and coils themselves around the trigger. Not a skill I've attained—yet.

The soft-brown-eyed probation officer giggled and asked, "Are you ready?"

I swallowed my pride, which only fed the butterflies, and said, "I guess."

"On the beep—BEEEP!"

My bipod, the competitive gunner's long-range crutch, and my handrail raked in and out of the slot edges splintering the plywood. My new battery only frustrated my efforts. The brightened reticle painted the plywood only eighteen inches in front of my face. Shifting my shooting angle so my eye peered through the slots, I clicked the trigger. She exclaimed my precision at 100 yards, "HIT! HIT! HIT!". A warm glow of glee rushed through my contorted body. My on-the-job training had me hitting targets left-handed, upside down, and blind. The round ended with a call of, "Time!", but in a really sweet voice.

The bad news was that missed shot penalties were mounting. The good news was that I didn't burn all my .223 bullets on the two remaining challenges of the stage. I moved on, running downrange past the first row of bat-tle-hardened steel infantry, their silver faces littered with hail damage from my shots. Sprinting past the red soldiers at the second challenge, self-disgust began to creep in as their freshly painted and shiny faces said it all.

In my head I cheered myself on, vowing "Make it back up on the run time to the next stage." I hollered back, "Thanks for being here. I'm having a blast!"

Running up the trail to the highest point of the club, I arrived at Stage Three. A tall skinny fellow wore a north woodsman's wool cap with drooping ears. His voice howled with a lingering drawl when he explained my objective. He said, "Two challenges; long range, free hand from a stair-case, um, leading to nowhere," as he pointed to the ob-stacles without looking up from the written script, "and a rooftop replica." The replica was in the shape of a cellar door, which is where my rank was headed if I didn't start shooting faster. With that, he started me with a beep.

Rising on the steps to nowhere, I gauged the flags waft-ing west in the wind and fired away. I aimed one target high. Then I shot down and left until I saw the metal swing and heard it ping. The metal sent an echo through the canyon at 200, 300 and 600 yards. The RO barked two "Hee-Yuts!"—hits, at each distance.

"Now I'm rocking what I got," I said to myself. My mind was standing and cheering. Next, I shifted to the rooftop replica challenge. For this, I lay prone and pulled my spring-loaded bipod legs down to act as support. Settled and ready to fire on the same targets, I was interrupted as the RO shouted, "Time!" I stopped cheering. My mind threw hope into the trash can as it mentally walked to the exit. Deflated and on my belly, I half rolled to one side. "What are we? Heating lunch in a microwave?"

The RO chuckled. "Well'sir. You did fine. No one has free-handed the 600s yet, and most use the staircase as a prop, not a podium." Obviously, you can't blame a guy for seeing his future. I was down to fifteen rifle bullets in my last mag, fifteen loose in my admin pouch, and I still hadn't unholstered my 9mm. I was off to Stage Four—how far away I had no idea.

I roller-coastered down and then back up the mountain. I scrambled through a cul-de-sac in the woods—the course designer probably dreamed it up in a carnival fun house. Finding my way out, I then hit the biggest water of the course. I plunged through the knee-deep creek and weaved blindly around head high peninsulas carved from the mud. Instead of slipping up and down the mud hills, I tried running around them. My trail shoes flooded with wet grime. After navigating the water, I hustled a half mile across a newly plowed field and climbed a wall someone put in the middle—probably the same guy that ran me in a demented circle in the woods. I made a mental note to provide feedback to management.

Just past the wall, Stage Four was alive with action. Gunfire popped as I approached. I showed clear actions to the attendant RO with an olive complexion and a mole just above the edge of his black cat hair mustache. On the other side of a safety berm, the sounds of both pistol and carbine fire raged. The RO slapped his hands together and exclaimed, "Welcome to Stage Four. No one times out on my stage. If you hear the beep, keep shooting. We want you to get better. While unholstering and holstering your handgun at 10-yard intervals out to 30-, you'll pull the weighted sled to each distance. The return will bring you back to 10 yards. Does the shooter understand the course of fire?"

"Yes!" and then I nailed it—not a single miss.

"You shoot like an Italian," the RO said without looking up from his scoring clipboard. Without offering me more, he welcomed the next shooter. With no time to spare, I dashed quickly to Stage 5.

I stopped and staggered—the sickness of the devious course planners had spread. It was a combo challenge with a VTAC board. Pistols on the left would save me— or not. At the VTAC board, I pinged four baseball-sized metal plates only a few feet away. "HIT! HIT! HIT! HIT!" announced the RO.

I scrambled over to the pistol challenge. I still had some mental momentum from Stage Four's smooth sailing. Then I promptly drowned in two 9mm magazines of missed shots on a pistol target at 20 yards. "Am I hitting anything?" I pleaded with the RO.

The stone-faced officer was entrenched in the rules and, thereby, entrusted with fairness. He said honestly, "Nope."

"Am I low? High?"

"That's on you," came the reply.

I tilted the handgun up forty-five degrees to check the weapon optic. It danced on top of the action like the lid on a diesel smoke stack. One screw was gone and the other holding the loose tooth of a scope. The sight jogged my memory as I recalled Jeff's fourth training tip, "Put blue Loctite on the green dot screws." I was jerked out of my opportunity to adjust my kit with a familiar refrain—"Time!"

I was panicked, but the emotionless RO spoke calmly. "Best to just remove the optic before you lose it on the next trail. Iron sights are fine for what we're doing." He turned on the lightbulb in my mind. It was a practical solution. The guy had just saved me half the cost of a rifle. I torque-wrenched the loose screw and dropped the optic in my admin bag. As I left Stage Five, I took a breath and hollered, "Thanks for being here. Having a great time!"

I was haggard, but hungry to leap-frog up the chain on the last run portion. I plodded back across the opposite edge of the plowed field, angling toward yellow tape. Hanging on a pine tree next to a wall of dirt, I saw the marked trail back up into the forest. Quickly looking around for a ladder for my ascent, but seeing none, I crawled and scraped up to a level spot. Bent over from effort, I yanked my head up and looked far above me through the pine tree pickets to see a snowy peak. The shade of the forest was quiet, disturbed only by my heaving exhaustion. I kept running higher on a soft bed of pine needles. To my surprise, the peak wasn't snow-covered. Instead, I had seen the sun lighting the paved road which cut our club in half—it was a road I wasn't allowed to use.

Sucking oxygen hard, I felt my lungs incinerating in a fiery furnace. At the far side of the plain, a traveling RO clapped as I approached. In obvious pride of trail design, he grinned and asked, "What did you think about that last hill?"

In a drooling huff, I blubbered, "You got issues, man. I prayed for your mortal soul the entire trip up."

The enthusiastic smile never left his face. We high-fived as I passed, and he said, "You're doing great. Almost finished. Stage Six is just behind me."

I entered Stage Six and showed clear. I was greeted by Paul, who I recognized from a distance by his glorious beard. He watched me behind a pair of my faces reflecting in his sunglasses. After reading the course of fire, he asked me to toss a hand grenade through a window to start the stage.

"WTF, Paul? A hand grenade?"

"It's not real, dumbass. Think I'd give you a live hand grenade? C'mon, man."

It was only a metal weight shaped like a hand grenade. It was probably fabricated by a 3-D printer hidden inside his enormous beard. I blazed through the zig-zag course, banging paper targets. Paul called out my time and shouted after me as I left, "Proud of ya'. You've come a long way in two months."

I shouted back. "Thanks, brother. Couldn't have done it without you guys."

I started sprinting with what energy I had left to trim seconds to the finish line. It was only a hundred yards up the hill. My pride and my chest began to blow out, the Velcro from my plate carrier coughing under the strain. I crossed a strip of duct tape to the applause of gathered ROs giving the same treatment to everyone. One shouted my time to the race director and commanded, "Show clear!" ...Gladly.

Victory is mine sayeth the finisher. Oh stopwatch, where art thou sting? My reward was a badass t-shirt, the contentment of trained performance, and correctable problems. The winner was the most unassuming father of two, who I met before the race. He beat everyone by four touchdowns. Think you can beat him? Gun up, get fit, and take your best shot—but don't take too long. Torture has a waitlist.

CRACKER

I used the last draw on my student loan for a bone-fishing trip in South Andros. I had become fearful my post-graduate textbooks would put a brick wall between me and my happiness. Yes, because as has been rumored, the best way to counteract the haunting memories of books is to engage in a battle of wits with bonefish.

Guide fees and plane tickets were only half the cost. I invested my portion of my recent divorce settlement on fishing gear. Our limited time together as husband and wife was just another sad story about burying relationship difficulties under a mountain of paper work. She was building her career. I was building mine.

My team partner at our bank, Murph, was also my classmate and emotional sensi. He convinced me bone fishing would smooth the speedbumps on love's rocky highway. "There's nothing here holding you back, Cracker," he said, as if fighting bonefish were some deep blue pool of emotional therapy.

There are a few things you need to know about Murph. He's as comfortable toasting champagne glasses at a commercial high rise grand opening as he is skinning a redfish with a borrowed knife under the deck of an oyster bar. He's purebred black-Irish from Savannah with a penchant for handing out nicknames. On a business trip to Singapore a few years earlier, I received mine. At that time, I was a pasty white ex-pat with locker room manners, hammering my way through cracked-pepper-crab. The inspirational scene in front of Murph was filled with sauce and crab parts spattering off the end of a metal hammer, swung by a nine-fingered American banker. Thus, my nickname was born. Without so much as a notary signature or a court appearance, Murph changed my name from Burrell to Cracker. It was fitting. I'd blown my ring finger off twenty-five years earlier one sunny Fourth of July. Ah, youth! Why is it wasted on the young?

Their stance in a landing pitch, the twin props roared as we flew lower over the gin-clear water. The pilot dropped the wheels and the plane set down lightly and taxied up to the small yellow cottage; Congo Town International Airport, South Andros, Bahamas. I couldn't help but notice the bubbly newlyweds a few rows up on the flight. They were stuck to one another like the glossy pages in a wedding album. The love birds were dressed in honeymoon fashion and smitten with new love. Murph was my current travel companion and always intuitive friend. He nudged my rib and whispered, "Are you going to ask them out on a date?"

"No," I huffed, because nothing says adventure like sulking over a dissolved marriage that emptied out like an office water cooler.

Waiting to deplane, my travelling anxiety around fly-fishermen emerged. My rod tube was four times longer than Murph's. It had carried my fishing rods from Venice to Miami. Only once had it been mistaken by security as a rocket-propelled grenade launcher. Murph's rods, on the other hand, were packaged in delicate little tubes attached to his backpack.

The guy leaning against one of the arrival vans had a pack identical to Murph's in style. He cleaned his fingernails with a fishhook and blew the debris from the point. He extended his hand from a rolled-up fisherman's sleeve. "I'm Dean. I guide in Wyoming."

We all wore grimaces of the fish-starved, partially hidden behind our wrap-around sunglasses. Dean's beard had a month's lead on ours. His wash-and-dry baseball cap, badged with a buffalo, covered a tangle of brown hair.

The introductions continued. "I'm Murph. This is Cracker."

"I'm Burrell Chetwick," I interjected. "Murph's just joking around."

With a dismissive nod and an air of superiority, Dean folded his arms and leaned back against the van. "I traded a couple of days with Lonnix. We caught big browns last month on the Snake River. His boy, Edwin, is guiding me this week on the flats."

Murph said with a disarming grin, "Last month Cracker and I served as adjutants to the US Embassy in Singapore, facilitated the merger of two small banks, and marked so high in finance class we skipped our MBA final."

The detailed story led Dean to believe we were titans of finance. Murph left out a large portion of the truth. We led the glamorous life of unpaid interns, reading local newspapers for the State Department. We briefed diplomats over Singapore Slings at the island nation's most exclusive country club. Indeed, both of the banks we worked for had merged during our brief assignments overseas. Upon return stateside, we volunteered for loan workouts and collections to keep ourselves from getting downsized. But, yes, we did skip the finance final. It didn't hurt that our professor shorted a supply-chain stock we theorized would tank. He retired the day of the test.

Edwin, the guide I had just learned about, was an oversized boy. He came from behind the van and stopped when he saw Murph. "Mr. Murph, welcome home!" In the fashion of the Bahamian street, he wore a micro-dry guide shirt, khaki pants and canvas shoes. His smile brightened as he approached. "Who's your friend?" he asked.

"My name's Burrell," I answered. "Can't wait to get started."

"Everyone calls him Cracker, Ed," Murph threw in for good measure.

I tried to cut him off before he got started. "No one calls me—"

"Cracka? Like Cracka-ass-cracka?" Edwin laughed.

"That's exactly right," Murph countered. His slap on Ed's back morphed into a man hug. "Good to see you!"

Edwin pried loose from Murph's hug and swooped down to collect our gear. While he dispatched the bags to the back of the van, he asked, "You ever fly-fish, Cracka?"

"That'd be the last time I fished for shellcrackers with a cane pole."

"Mercy me! You da' real bream busta?" His pearly whites were testing the limits of my sunglasses' UV protection.

Dean looked at my rod tube and asked, "What's in the bazooka?"

"Big-fish rods and reels," I said, hopeful fly-fishermen weren't as stuffy as I'd heard.

"You brought spinning reels and pier rods!? For Bonefish?" There it was.

I twirled the bazooka in my left hand, minus a ring finger. Edwin loaded it in the van. Then I gave Dean my awkward, but signature, thumbs up, showcasing my missing piece. I thought I laughed alone, until I saw Murph chuckling as he stood by the front door of the van.

The sand-beaten van teetered out onto the pavement. We passed the newlyweds motoring in the opposite direction. Their transport was a polished SUV with a resort decal plastered on the side. The logo had a pool and a spa—no bonefish. They had no idea what they were missing.

The potholes in the coral road rocked the van from side to side. The sweet rhythm of reggae broadcast with a moderate amount of static from the speakers. Sweat ran down my back, sticking my shirt to the vinyl seat. The radio station faded out as we reached the bleached-white southern tip of South Andros—Mar's Bay. Purple clouds floated above the water surface. The horizon was as faint as a thin paint stroke. Triggered by the setting sun, a swarm of gnats burrowed into my ankles and fed.

The van slowed and then stopped. A tall man with a confident look walked from behind a row of blockhouses. His jaws and forehead formed a square. He was large and round. His crossed arms rested on his chest and twisted together into one. The gnarled root shape was sheathed in the same style micro-dry guide shirt rolled up to his elbows we all wore. His was weathered by the sun; mine by the rinse cycle of the first wash. The generational resemblance to Edwin was clear. He opened his palms and welcomed us as the consummate resort host. "Murph and Dean, welcome home." They hugged and slapped each other's backs. He smiled at me and said, "And you must be Burrell."

"I am."

Murph exclaimed on cue, "Call him Cracker, Lonnix."

"Here we go again," I said, accepting my fate.

Lonnix turned to face the storm offshore and pointed to the beach, his arm as if a sledgehammer. "Da wind is out of da southeast. Da waves on dis side are high all da way to da flats. We pray for northwest winds. We prayed for dem last week, too, but da weatherman say God don answer 'yes' til you leave." The stiff wind blowing our hats loose was conspicuously absent from the travel brochures.

Our bonefish adventure began with a weather question-mark. On day two, we received an answer to our prayers for calm winds—and it was still a no. The wind howled, but no matter. The price of the boat ride was paid. We tossed safety into a tornado and launched from a place called Pleasant Bay that was anything but. Edwin and Dean sat in the skiff next to us, bouncing from the incoming surf and waiting on Lonnix's first move.

Lonnix stood in the stern behind us, an in-person version of what every man wanted to be—a veritable Caribbean statue. Murph and I strapped and buckled ourselves into the two center seats. Three fly rods wobbled in their horizontal mounts strapped under the boat's side lip. Lonnix had a working model, Murph's was engraved, and mine still shone like a new tool I had no idea how to use. All our rods were lined for big bonefish and flied with Murph's original bone crushers he'd tied himself.

My pier rod was mounted in the rod holder on the opposite side, sprouting from the boat gunnel like a radio antenna. On the black foam handle was a barrel of green fishing line wrapped on a spool. The crank was larger than the handle on a roll-up car window. The taut line bent the rod backward as it fed up through the rod-eyes, and ended with a feathered steel hook in the tip. The oversized bail burst forward from the rod emulating the closed fist of a gearhead's thumbs-up. The rod shaft; limber as a billy-club.

Lonnix shouted out over the outboard. "Hold on! We gon to get the big bones!" He twisted the throttle and we sped forward. Murph and I turned our hat-bills around to keep them from blowing off. Edwin's boat vanished behind us.

Our outboard whined as the plywood missile of a boat shot into the South Andros gust. The churning green water met the bow with a repeating slap. The pounding reverberated faster and faster, eventually morphing to airborne taps. Lonnix had pushed the throttle as far is it would go. The big wave tops, detached by the wind, poured over the gunnels. I was soaked.

In a discreet attempt at relief, I turned back to our intrepid captain, only to panic at the water rising around his ankles. He bent his bouncing knees and pulled the skiff's drain plug with his free hand. The flood waters swirled through the tiny hole, returning it to whence it came.

Almost losing my grip from the jarring motion, I looked forward to the sloppy saltwater wilderness before me. My faith in man dwindled.

We soon rounded a coral encased peninsula. The rough ride subsided and I sighed in relief and released my knuckle's grip on the seat bottom. An amazing emerald green flat spread out before us. The white caps were no more. In their place was a clear glass landscape, with innumerable cays, inland swamps, and white sand. No other men nor machine were in sight. Underwater gullies, channels and drop-offs undulated below the skiff, now skimming on a shallow sea of glass.

Taking the first moment to breath and wipe the water from my eyes, I twisted around and asked Lonnix, "Do most of your fisherman drown?"

He laughed. "Not dat I remember. We'll peel around dis flat and start walkin."

"How far we walking?" Murph asked.

"Two, maybe tree' miles."

I retched in combination with the chill running down my spine.

Murph raised his eyebrows, "You okay, Cracker?"

"What?" I tried to whisper. "No! Did he say two or three miles?" Lonnix's web page was loaded with big fish pictures, but suggested no pre-trip physical training nor the constant wind advisories. Such is the flashy lure of adventure.

The bill of Lonnix's hat was longer than average, which made the cap sitting askew on his head seem smaller. With his long and level arm he pointed toward the salt grass. "We'll work these three coves," he said, gesturing to basins that stretched wide before us. "Those gullies in each bay drain cold water into da main channel. We'll park da boat here and circle back."

Murph hopped down onto the sandy bottom and stuffed a wad of tobacco in his cheek. He shoved the pouch in his shirt pocket and looked at me. "Want some?"

I retched again. "No. I'm good."

Murph took his flyrod from Lonnix's outstretched hand and held it parallel with the water. His shirttails floated around his belt. He tapped the shaft above the reel, and his fly dropped onto the water below his rod. The tiny hook, wrapped in handtied threads, was hidden and ready to grab anything that dared bite it. Murph articulated his wrist, causing the fly to twitch like a live shrimp, clicking in escape. As he waded away from the boat, his torso rotated with his hands held high. Murph walked with his bonecrusher fly in one hand, rod in the other.

Lonnix wasted the next three hours teaching me. "Let the rod do da work, Cracka" was all I remember about the lessons. Within a couple of hours, I was double-hauling and false-casting fly line with the confidence of a unicycle-rider twisting hoops on his arms. Silver flashes of bonefish, the same color as sand, occasionally appeared by chance at the end of my false-cast. My form was of no use. The shadow of my fly darkening the sandy bottom scattered the nursery bone fish, along with my hopes.

After a long march through the first two coves, I hiked into the third. "Doing any good?" Murph hollered from a distance ahead of me.

Before I could say anything, Lonnix reported back, "Strugglin!" Lonnix noticed my sideways glance before I did. "Check your tippet," he said. The tippet is a thinner length of line at the very end of the leader that encourages the fly to float and swim more naturally in the water. "It's pearled with wind knots from the hook to the tippet splice." He stood patient and removed, several yards away from me in the water.

Running my fingers along the tippet's line, I felt the bumps of the knots, cursing every second they would take to untie. Inescapable proof of my casting over-enthusiasm, I was deflated. "Damn it, Lonnix! Why does this keep happening?" I blamed the sport for my lack of experience. Rubber-boot-stomping through miles of mud and sand had worn blisters on my ankles. The itch of the mosquito scars burned my skin. My legs were beginning to give out.

Ignoring the extent of my suffering, Lonnix pointed with discovery. "Big bones. Two of em'! See em', Murph?"

I hurried in vain to untangle the wind knots in order to get my shot. Murph raised his rod to vertical, the fly line looping behind him. His bonecrusher fly, nearly invisible on the clear tippet, reached the apex of the back-cast. Murph dropped his forearm to bring it forward for the false-cast once, back, and then forward again. The stripped line that had piled on the water's surface rose through the rod-eyes. The rising line shot the fly to a spot just ahead of the two shadows, moving back and forth along the bottom.

Murph's outstretched arms stiffened to a pause. One of the shadows altered its course, then both. They neared the bright floating line when Murph gently lifted his rod. "Fish on!" he yelled. He leaned back, the reel screaming in his hand as the fish pulled on the line.

Lonnix pointed his finger at the second fish breaking across our path. "Cracka! Here he comes. Out in front of him. Like we practiced."

"Wind knots or no wind knots, there ain't no refunds," I thought out loud. I double-hauled the line in preparation for final delivery. On my second false-cast, a gust of wind blew a spaghetti pile of fishing line into my face. It was a missed opportunity. I grimaced and felt my hands shaking. "I need a moment. I'll be over here," as I walked away into an imagined privacy.

Murph's fish fled to the seagrass, but he steadied the tightening line. The bonefish made a few more runs and, exhausted from hook and haul, surrendered. With casual grace, Murph slowly walked over to cradle his prize. My ex-wife bought me a waterproof camera for our first Christmas. I pulled it out and played my supporting role, snapping a few shots of Murph as he pinched the little hook from the fish's jaw. He opened his palms and the fish swam free.

Lonnix's voiced his approval: "Murph was born to it." Then he looked at me and said, grinning, "You could do dat one day, Cracka." He readjusted the bill of his hat and clarified, "Many, many days from now."

Murph performed the delicate dance of the fly fisherman as he caught two more the same way. He was casting to shadows imprinted on the coral and tightening line to the world's spookiest fish. After we hopped in the boat, Murph picked up a bottle of water rolling on the boat floor and drank it. I was too disgusted with myself to think about hydration. Murph looked back to Lonnix. "Where to now, boss?"

Standing tall and gripping the outboard throttle for support, Lonnix said, "We gon to let Cracka eat. Gon to a blue hole."

My spirits soared as I looked back. His smile spread into the pinpoints of his dimples. He said, "I thought you might like dat."

Murph asked, "How far?"

"Two, maybe tree' miles." Lonnix twisted the throttle and we sped across the open expanse of sea.

Racing across the glass, we saw a dark dot hovering on the surface in the distance. After a few minutes, the dot grew to the size of a football field, but perfectly round. The boat idled over the top of a giant blue hole. All the way around the submerged border, rocks dusted with sand in gravity's grasp defined the edge of the abyss. We floated inside the circle, halfway between the edge and the center. Shadows below us either writhed in slow motion or appeared motionless as torpedoes lying in wait.

Lonnix turned the boat so we all faced the edge. He touched the throttle intermittently to keep us positioned. "Go ahead, Cracka. What you waiting for?" he said.

I unleashed my redemption, my spinning rod. Yanking it from its holder, I clicked the bale open. The jig dangled on the rod tip from my fingered trigger on the green fishing line.

Lonnix pointed to the edge and encouraged me. "Sling your jig near the gulley. See the bones circling?" A jagged notch appeared at the rim's edge several feet underwater.

Murph looked to where Lonnix pointed. "Those are the biggest bonefish I've ever seen!" He sat down on the bow. "Cracker, you don't see that cloud of pink dust?"

Wild with anticipation, I admitted, "Nope, but that don't matter. Time to let the big dog eat." I twitched the stiff rod in reverse and loaded the steel jig with energy. My top hand whipped forward with the power of a framing hammer, pulling my bottom hand backward with the same energy, minus a ring finger. I plucked the green line as the rod tip lofted the shanked lure. A gusting tailwind arced the path until the lure landed with grace precisely on target. A small bump on my fingertip signaled it rested on the bottom. I began heaving the rod and working the jig, reeling slack as I dropped the rod tip.

"Perfect," Lonnix encouraged. "Jig! Jig! Jig! They're after it."

Then came the moment of truth. As reliable as lady luck, shadows formed into a triangle and the bones moved toward the seafloor. "Jig! Jig! Jig!" Lonnie demanded.

The lure bounced into our view—the invisible string of the clear tippet pulling it off the bottom. I gave the rod a solid haul. The jig head jumped from the seafloor, over the rim's edge and dove into the abyss of the blue hole. Following the feathers, the bonefish raced and maneuvered.

Bursting to the front of a scattering starburst of shadows, a bonefish inhaled the sinking jig. I heaved my rod and couldn't believe my luck. "I'm hooked up!" My reel-drag screamed its cheerful sound. The end of the green line disappeared back up onto the flat.

Now the drama unfolded. A blue and black torpedo, evolved to serve a mouthful of knives, shot up from the abyss. In a streak, a barracuda decapitated one of the retreating bonefish. The prey's blood trail clouded the water. Murph said, "Whoa! Sliced in half." My line was still tight to a live one.

Lonnix yelled, "Hold on! You hooked up to da whale bone!"

My fear hit another gear when I noticed the metal of my reel unveiled by the spooling line. Suddenly, the drag silenced. The green line, taught with tension, stopped spooling and I began to work.

Lonnix yelled, "You gettin enough action, Cracka?"

"Absolutely!" I shouted out at the moment. "She's a good one, but I might not have enough reel."

Murph stood for the action, whacked my back and hollered, "I got confidence in you. Your reel's plenty big."

The fish understood with clarity it's coming death and jerked and fought to hold tight on the flat. After a few minutes, worn and weary from my reel drag, the bonefish shot straight for the boat. Another blue and black barracuda erupted from the deep. Like a guillotine slicing the water, it ran up through the bonefish and breached the water's surface. It leapt toward our skiff while twitching its tail, and came face to face with Murph. At that point, events became a little fuzzy.

Murph sprung into a backflip to dodge the barracuda. He was given a boost by a wave lifting the bow of the boat. His knees tucked to bring his feet to twelve o'clock, effecting the visual of propelling the fish through an aerial somersault. Murph and the barracuda flung through the air with the grace of a trapeze tandem.

Murph's feet came around to six o'clock and hit the water. His head disappeared and made a small splash. He popped up to face us, his cap floating next to the boat. Throwing his head from side to side, he attempted to triage anything bleeding. All that motion and flesh in the water attracted more uninvited company. Four barracudas, their jaws dripping teeth, surrounded him and gazed like predators looking at dinner.

Lonnix screamed, "Get in da boat before they take you to da bottom! It's not a democracy down der!"

Murph lifted himself over the side of the boat. The barracudas which had been lying in wait simply floated back out of sight. Lonnix threw my saltwater trophy of a halved barracuda out and began washing down the boat. Thankfully, there was none of Murph's blood to mix with the sea water on the boat deck.

The moment had drained me, mentally and physically. The heat from the sun landed on my forehead. I sat down to take it all in, fell back and was helpless as my eyes closed...

I awoke to small ripples lapping up on the beach at Lonnix's place. The bursting colors across the sunset sky glowed on the wall of the fish shack. Murph's voice brought me to full consciousness. "Welcome back to the living, Burrell. How do you feel?"

Pushing back into the beach chair, my dry mouth crackled, "What happened?"

"You passed out," Edwin said, coming from behind the weathered hut with a six-pack of beer. He replaced the group's empties and handed one to me. "Dis probably won't help, but it definitely won't hurt. Next time, don pass out. I had to carry you from da van."

"Sorry about that," I said, embarrassed. I tilted the bottle neck and took a good swallow, bubbles thundering up to the bottom of the glass.

Water gurgled from behind the bar as Lonnix cleaned the salt from the reels. His voice boomed from the hut's rear quarter next to the beer boxes. "You like da salt of da earth, Cracka." The group roared with laughter after he finished. "A little go a long way."

I raised my beer bottle on the back of my hand, the long-neck cradled in my nub and cheered, "To bonefish!"

The beer bottles clinked as my head spin slowed to a controlled wobble.

Lonnix patted Edwin on the back. "I leave you boys to it. Transport to Congo Town International will be here at six a.m."

The Caribbean dusk filled the sky with darkening colors, and we spun lies for hours. We found our way back to bed by starlight.

The next morning as we boarded the plane back to Atlanta, I couldn't help but chuckle at the newlyweds climbing the stairs before us. Pausing a moment at the top of the gangway, the movie-star bride turned to take a parting gaze at paradise. In a starlet's mockery of fishing escapades, she winked at us before she swatted her new husband on the flank.

I felt a pang in my side. Murph removed his elbow from my rib, and smiled. "She ain't strugglin with wind knots."

LE TIGRE

Jessica and Elliot were married in Hollywood style. A-list celebrities fawned over the magical couple, and danced all night at their wedding. Jessica was molded by the world's best private schools. She had podiumed as a member of the Olympic swim team multiple times. Elliot, a club champion in his own right, was the CEO of an international insurance company. His notoriety in Paris was so widespread, the President of France nicknamed him Le Tigre.

The couple's fifteen-year age difference—Jessica a mere twenty something on their wedding day—seemed inconsequential in the beginning. As the years passed, Elliot wasn't so sure.

Elliot was tall, slender and certified Ivy League. He was well manicured, with thick black hair that flowed just so to the back of his head. Today he sat next to Justin on the tennis court bench, wiping his brow with a crisp club towel. Justin's rugged good looks could headline any western movie or adventure film with an Oscar budget. They were both dressed in their best whites.

Justin turned to Elliot and asked, "Where's Jessica?"

Elliot replied "I sent her down to the Bahamas a month ago to close on our fourth home. We needed a beach getaway within a three-hour jet ride from work." He put a period to his statement with a drink from his sparkling water bottle.

"You sent her alone? Will she be okay by herself? Remember, I knew her before I introduced you two."

"Of course she's okay. I gave her a ski chalet in the Alps, an ocean front surf shack in SoCal, and a monthly allowance larger than the GDP of most small countries. She's sweating diamonds, Justin. Isn't that what all trophy wives want?"

"Whatever you say," Justin said. "Isn't that a lot of cash flow hassle?"

"Not really. My firm owns all the houses and the cars so I don't have to keep up with the mortgages." Shifting gears, Elliot mused, "Funny you should mention it, though. She asked me to support her as she begins to explore herself."

Justin sat upright against the bench back and asked, "Are you invited on this little journey, or can just anyone tag along?"

"If, by anyone, you mean someone that can support her lifestyle, he or she, should bring along a bank vault," he chuckled. "She wants me to be more adventurous. She might tone it down if she saw me working a boardroom in Europe. My God, my travel schedule is getting worse."

"You say that every year," Justin said. With his club towel hanging from his hands, he lolled his head back behind the bench and continued. "This might seem a strange suggestion, old friend, but the director at one of my first auditions told me to toughen up. He said I should read Hemingway. The first brawler I played was the twin of Eddy from Islands in the Stream. It's how I got the part."

"This is my wife, Justin. I'm not much of an actor. I'm one of the richest men on the planet. That's why she married me."

"Sure, El. Money talks. That's what I say."

A few days later, Elliot was on the corporate jet, talking over the phone with Jessica. She said from land, "You'll love this island, Elliot. With a private air strip and a full staff, I stole this compound."

"Well, hopefully, the police aren't there to arrest me when I arrive."

Insulted, Jessica replied, "That's what I mean. You don't think I can do anything right."

"I didn't mean..." Elloitt stammered right before she hung up. Harried from the deal he'd just closed on the NATO military, Le Tigre was weary. He let his eyes rest on the clouds below him as they floated by. Trying to relax, he picked up Hemingway's short stories on his seat console. Justin had given him his personal copy as a token of friendship. He dogeared The Short Happy Life of Francis Macomber, a story among many—but Elliot didn't start anything in the middle. His brain worked from beginning to end, just as he competed in business and in life. He flipped through a few pages and was almost asleep when the wheels touched down.

A white truck with oversized tires and an open top came racing out on the tarmac to meet the jet. Jessica's brown hair was blowing above the roll bar, but he couldn't place the man in the driver's seat. As he stepped off the plane, Jessica jumped from the doorless vehicle and ran to him. Throwing her arms around his neck, she proclaimed, "All for us!"

"Who's us," Justin asked. He watched the tan lanky young man at the wheel. He was smiling and wearing a red tank top with a white cross on the front.

"Oh, that's just Arnaud. He owns the dive shop on the island. I've been getting ready so I can take you."

"I was hoping for tennis and golf," he said, looking into her eyes.

"Well, that'll have to wait," she said. "I picked this island because it doesn't have any of those dull sports—if you can call those sports."

Elliot walked toward the truck with Jessica in tow, hand in hand. He asserted his authority, calling to Arnaud, "Hey Frenchy. Pleasure to meet you. My bags are at the top of the stairs." The command to the driver-turned-bellhop was explicitly implied. He stood at the hood of the truck to ensure his directive was heard.

Arnaud said, "I'm not a valet, Elliot. It's nice to meet you, too."

Jessica intervened, "Please Arnaud. Elliot's only her for a few days."

Arnaud walked past them both to the jet gangway, while Elliot got in the driver's seat. Jessica took note of Elliot's change. She'd hoped it would come with a wedding ring, but had never appeared.

Lugging the suitcases to the truck, he dropped them in the bed and said, "I didn't think you drove yourself anywhere, Le Tigre."

"Only presidents and prime ministers call me that, Arnaud. I'm on vacation. Get in. Let's have some fun," Elliot said. He watched an eye exchange between his wife and the dive instructor in the rearview mirror. He tossed his book next to the gear shifter and grabbed Jessica's knee. With a firm grip, he leaned over and kissed her on the cheek and whispered. "So glad I'm here. I wouldn't want to miss the exploration."

That night the couple—now a trio—met the local expats at a beachside restaurant. Elliot knew the type and tagged them immediately as a subset of beneficiaries. Glowing with a Caribbean view of the water and soft lights strung from the rafters, the open-air restaurant would normally be a place of reprieve.

With tension building in his chest, Elliot gazed over the open knit tops and short skirts of Jessica's new girlfriends. Arnaud brought some of his dive crew along. He probably expected Elliot to pay. He would, of course. The CEO paid for every group he'd ever called friends. Munching on conch appetizers and drinking Bahama mamas by the pitcher, Elliot struck up a conversation with the dive crew.

"What keeps you boys busy," he asked of the tanned dive masters.

"Not much," a dive instructor with an English accent admitted. "We dive when Arnaud gets a high-end client, but we're so far from the big islands, not much business comes this way."

Another spoke up in an Australian accent, "I think Arnaud likes it that way. For me, I came for the rich Sheilas that fly in." As soon as he said it, he demurred, "Oh, I didn't mean Jessica and the like," but Elliot knew he did.

Elliot glanced over to see Jessica whispering something in Arnaud's ear, his blond curls lifted above his ear by her hand.

The English dive instructor grabbed his arm and said, "Jessica said you're scuba certified?"

"I am," Elliot said, frustrated.

"Good. Jessica signed you both up for a shark dive tomorrow. We're all going."

"Well, it's been a few years," Elliot said, opening himself up to the hope of a sea adventure.

The Australian grunted, "Not a deal breaker. We're only about fifty feet deep. Sharks everywhere. You can sit on your knees and watch the show."

"There's another group in from New York, so it's a full trip," English said. They're sitting at the table over by the bar," and nodded in that direction. "See the smoke show at the end of the table?"

Elliot, distracted that he was not a part of the conversation between his wife and Arnaud, said, "Yeah, sure."

"She's an oil heiress. She pays for the whole family to come down every year."

The Australian grunted, "First opportunity, her and I are going to drill."

The Englishman shot back, "You're insane. You'll be the last bloke to bed that woman."

The Australian shrugged and tilted up his beer bottle.

Dusk turned to night. Elliot's hectic schedule of the previous few days caught up to his eyelids. He paid for the party to continue and said good night to everyone. "Jessica, you coming with me?"

"No, I'll stay a little longer. These are new friends and we're just getting acquainted."

"Fine. I've a few more calls to make and a book to finish." He took one last sip of his tropical drink and said, "Be ready, though, tomorrow we dive with the sharks."

"Oh, you're going," she asked, surprised.

"Why wouldn't I? I swim with them every day in the office." His grin gave evidence that he spoke the truth.

Arnaud reached across Jessica's back as if to embrace her, but then opened his hand to shake Elliot's. He was ignored. As Elliott passed the bar, the dark beauty from New York with onyx eyes looked up from her own group and glanced at him. He wondered briefly of her story as he left.

The next morning, the crew from last night could be found checking air tanks and dive equipment while Elliot and Jessica looked on, silently. A bit hungover, Jessica asked, "Do you like everyone's swimsuits?" The dive crew sported the same expensive bikinis, but in different colors. The men's briefs were as small as the women's. In an odd coincidence, Arnaud's and Jessica's were the same color.

Elliot remarked, "Make sure and ask me before you spend my money on a swimsuit for me. I'm fine with board-shorts."

"What's wrong? You don't like them," she asked.

"Jessica, you've turned them into trained seals."

"Are you jealous?"

"Hardly."

Arnaud had everyone from New York sign waivers and then handed a clipboard to Elliot. "This is the waiver."

"Thanks, Arnaud. I'm in the business. I'll sign it, but if anything happens to me, you're screwed in at least two countries and maybe by a couple of high-end military operators."

"Nothing's going to happen. I've been training these sharks since I arrived."

"That so? We'll see."

Jessica huffed, "Can we all just enjoy this?"

Arnaud and Elliot both answered at the same time, "Sure," and "Of course, dear."

Elliot noticed the dark New York beauty, wearing a tastefully sheer one piece, staring at their awkwardness. In the stern by the motors, the Australian was staring at him.

Air tanks and dive gear were stacked in the center of the boat between the dive benches. Excitement lit up the faces of the New Yorkers as the dive boat pushed through the waves toward the dive site. A teen girl shouted across the boat to Jessica, "Can you believe it? Swimming with tiger sharks? How could we get this lucky?"

Jessica, thinking of something else, said, "I asked for it. How about you?"

"Oh yeah. Definitely," she replied. "This is my graduation present from Aunt Zhara." The dark beauty smiled and bowed her head toward Jessica.

Jessica shook her head, as Elliot sat stoically, considering whether he'd make it back to land.

The boat arrived at a seemingly arbitrary spot in the water. Hovering above the dive site, Arnaud gave his assistants instructions and briefed everyone on what to expect. There were thorough warnings against quick movements, and for keeping your arms folded in front of you. He'd write the species on a clip board as they came around for identification to use in their stories back home.

And with that, having been equipped and tested, all the divers fell in backwards over the sides of the boat and met at the bottom. They gathered on their knees in a ring.

Ropes of tiny bubbles rose from their masks, connecting them to the surface, dissected by shafts of the sun's rays.

The Englishman and the other dive instructors interspersed themselves within the ring. Jessica knelt next to Elliot. Working in a flurry on the edge of the ring, Arnaud and the Australian began pulling fish entrails, cut and whole, from a tangle of floating milk crates. The chum made the water milky.

The Pavlovian sharks came fast. While the Australian fed, Arnaud scribbled in grease pen on the white board, "Lemon." A different species, with anchor shaped noses, cruised by engulfing fish. Arnaud drew a hammer on the white board and showed the group the picture. A few divers laughed bubble rings.

Grouper, as large as the sharks and unphased by fear, darted in and out of the water column gobbling up chunks. Elliot, enjoying himself, noticed a couple of large shapes on the edge of visibility. Arnaud saw them at the same time and peered over to Elliot. As they circled closer, the stripes on their sides needed no identification. The massive beasts swam on the back side of the ring as Jessica began to point.

Elliot tried to knock her hands down. He felt her resist, as if she was turning everyone's attention towards the Tigers and away from Arnaud. In the moment, Elliot looked to Arnaud, who was smiling around his mouthpiece as he held up the board for only him to see. It read, Le Tigre. On cue, the Australian launched a whole tuna in Elliot's direction. Both beasts tacked toward the bait, now coming directly for Elliot. Swimming over the top of the circle, their enormous length and girth dwarfed anything else—the size of three people.

Jessica was still pointing. The current from her waving hand drew the bait's trajectory away from Elliot and into her body. It happened in an instant. In a single bite, her torso was gone. The half mannequin in a bikini bottom tilted forward into the sand. Arnaud's eyes went wide in horror. Everyone in the ring watched in shock. The second tiger came in and shook a leg free of the heap. The feeding frenzy, now in full swarm, cleaned up the mess. Cough bubbles came from the onlookers, who began to sicken into their mouthpieces. Fearing they'd also be attacked they could only watch helplessly and remain motionless until the danger had passed.

Elliot's emotions churned from thankfulness to regret. He finished in scorn. He and Arnaud stared at one another through the bloody water.

After a time, the group floated back to the surface. They assembled back on the boat. The young graduate relieved her sickness over the rail. Female divers were crying and wailing. The Englishman was stoic. Arnaud prattled into the radio for help, useless as that was. The Australian showed no emotion as he collected gear and stowed it away for the trip back. Understanding the lawlessness of paradise, Elliot held his tongue. And he planned his revenge.

Zhara looked on quietly, until she could contain herself no more. Near the dock, she moved to sit in the empty spot next to Elliot. Her wet black hair fell in ringlets around her shoulders. Dripping onto her chest above the sheer swimsuit, the Arabian ends floated on the wind. She leaned in and whispered to Elliot in her soft but distinct Middle Eastern accent, "She deserved it."

Jetting back to the mainland, Zhara thumbed through Elliot's book. He talked on the phone and she listened quietly as he returned his insurance policy to original status from its recent change only days ago—the denial of claim by shark attack. She touched his hand approvingly when he described Arnaud and the Australian to another person and offered his compound as a "center of operations."

He powered the phone off. The steward approached and he ordered a glass of champagne. Nodding to Zhara, he asked, "Would you like anything?"

She replied, "I have everything I want." Her sharpened smile held him in a trance. "Except for maybe one thing."

WELCOME HOME
NICK THORNE

Lynton, England • Spring 1944

The damage done, I lay amidst the shadows of our library. I had returned home from the British Middle East Command to Exmoor without solace. Father was no more. Mother had grown exhausted from the chaos of London's overcrowded hospital, the war-torn mortar of its walls eroding with every blitz from Hitler's Luftwaffe. She brought me home to our ancestral estate on the Bristol Channel. My inherited skills, refined under Father's tutelage and tested on the battlegrounds, played a crucial role in securing the Allied victory in the Second War.

Father, an old comrade of Prime Minister Churchill, had been enlisted for Operation Countenance. It was a joint operation with the Russians. The objective; expelling the Germans from Iran. Father accepted for both of us. His experience was known only in the memories of England's war ministry and the station reports from Germany's Gestapo. He intertwined secret service to the Crown with an archaeological facade, and revealed ancient political secrets buried beneath the Arabian desert. Dispatched in the summer of 1941, our mission aimed to reach Tehran while clearing bridges and tunnels along the Trans-Iranian Railway. That treacherous journey had led me here, where I lay in a deep sleep. The trauma of a saboteur's raid wrecked my dreams of peace and home.

In the dimly lit library, a plump nurse attended to me. Elle, as she was known, marked by the weight of her arms and the clean scent of alcohol, left mother, Angus and I alone after tea, as she had done every day since my arrival. I heard the old English door creak and felt a rush of cold air on her departure. "If you see any change in Sir Nicholas, please ring for me," she instructed. "Try to get some rest, mum. We might be in for a very long ordeal."

Mother bade her farewell, invoking the resilience of the Thorne lineage. "Thank you, Elle. We'll be fine. The Thornes' constitution is stronger than the oak in your hand."

"Yes, mum," Elle said, and closed the door.

With that, the room was left to the whispers of history and the weight of familial secrets.

My recovery was to take place in the massive library, amid Father's collection of ancient tomes and scrolls. The bay window framed the long open moor stretching down to the coast, guarded by the long guns of the British Navy. From our early years, Angus and I had explored the room's enchanting mysteries, captivated by tales of magic and prophecy.

The cushion of Mother's leather chair crackled and wheezed. Air inflated her empty seat as she stood, and I felt her touch on my hand, a fleeting reassurance. "Son, I love you," she said, kissing my cheek. Then she returned to her place and drifted back to her own dreams. Angus, a comforting presence, broke the silence with his deep voice, expressing his loneliness and the changing dynamics of our home. Off in the distance, falling bombs rumbled across the forested land and shook the windows.

"Seems I've brought the war back with me, Angus," I started, searching in my darkness for an old friend.

"Afraid it never left," he said, the deep bass in his voice soothing my sorrow. "We're keeping up the enthusiasm to defeat Hitler, but the training and blasting in the forest is hard on my peace, and the dining room settings. I suppose it's better than being bombed by the enemy."

"Father and I sent protests to His Majesty and the Prime Minister, requesting the training cease. We reasoned the war and the red stag's end would coincide should the games continue, not to mention the added burden of yours' and Mother's distress. They both replied, to our family's credit, but in the negative. Chin up, ole' boy. Hitler's on the run. It won't be long now."

"The bombs echo from the cliff faces, Nick, shaking the chandeliers. After a big grand slam, I have to alert Mother of broken glass on the ballroom floor."

No stranger to sleepless nights, my eyes had burned in the wee hours from the bombs' flashing on the North African front. The lack of concern I had for family back home now swung to empathy. "I'm sorry you and mother had to endure that. I dare say your ears ring louder than mine, as close to the action as you are, out here in Exmoor."

"It's not much like the home you remember, Nick," Angus said with a voice of melancholy. "The Celtic ponies and red stag are all gone."

"They'll come back," I said with hope.

"Only God knows. I don't think about them when you're not here."

Our conversation meandered through memories of a bygone era. I shared the tale of Father and my journey in the Persian theatre of war. The library's air was a cocoon, nurturing the unfolding narrative, weaving through the landscapes of Iran, the bridges of the Trans-Iranian Railway and the bonds forged in the crucible of war.

After some time, I broached the subject we both wanted to rehash, but hadn't yet come to grips. "When did you find out Father died?" I asked Angus.

Angus stood up from his chair, paced a bit, and then sat down again. "A chap from the RAF came up to tell Mother. She showed a stiff upper lip when he handed her Father's Distinguished Flying Cross. She did, that is, until he briefed her on your condition in the hospital. Then she came undone," he sniffled. "So did I."

"Thank God you were here, Angus," I said in consolation, knowing he chafed from his absence from the service. When Father and I left for foreign shores, Angus had begged me for passage. Left out of the planning, he went hunting the day we shipped out.

Angus answered, "I wonder sometimes, did God leave me here, or did the devil convince me to stay? Either way, Nick, I'm worn by more than the years, and I'm sure Mother feels the same." He sighed loud enough for me to hear again.

"So too with me, Angus," I said, trying to sooth his simmering tension.

I absorbed the inkling of our growing esprit décor I'd been without for so long. Now I muscled up my courage, but still hesitated. "I need to tell you something, Angus. It's about the war."

"I've imagined you dead so many times, I know of no worse burden I could bear," Angus moaned. "Please, humor me with your story."

I began the account I longed to share, but until now, didn't have the strength. "We sailed on the HMS Yarra into the port of Bandar Shahpour as part of Operation Marmalade in August of 1941. Father, I and the Indian Army sailed the Yarra, up the river Shaat Al-Arab. We were the tip of the spear, with the determination to run the Nazis through. These were summer nights under the starry sky of the Persian Gulf. It was sweltering."

The smoke of bombs in my memory began to clear. "I stepped in behind the Yarra's port side four-inch-gun for the attack on the Iranian Navy docked at Khorramshahr. Father checked the Indian commandos gear and charged their resolve. He coaxed anxiety from its hold on the soldiers, shouting confidence into their spirit and glaring fearlessness into their souls. Once nutters and one-off liquidizers chased out of India by bank overdrafts and prison wardens, he elevated them into a battle-ready mob. He prepared them to board a ship and cease it."

Angus was enthused. "Always aim high, Nick. You remember what I told you?"

"I remember. You would've been proud, ole' boy. We prowled behind a British merchant ship in the dark and freed the gun barrels on her port side. To our grand luck, we came upon the Babr, the largest gunboat the Iranians could afford. We were so close; I had to eyeball my target. On the second hand of Operation Marmalade's synchronized commencement, I began firing at the ship, sitting like a duck tied to the harbor. Boom! Boom! Boom! In seconds, the hot shells pealed her metal back from stem to stern. We were in the pitch."

"Crack shot!" barked Angus.

"Shocked from their bunks, the Iranian Nazis watched from the dock's side as the Babr's bridge settled into the water. The ropes connecting the hull to the harbor's wooden cleats snapped like rubber bands, stretched beyond their limit.

"Father commanded the first landing party into the ship-to-shore boat that disembarked from the Yarra. I unfolded from the gun turret in the nick of time and jumped into the second boat speeding away, my rope and grappling hook hanging from my shoulder. We rallied the Indian commandos, ace volunteer savages, and hurled the flying-hooks onboard every enemy vessel in the harbor. We climbed hand-over-hand. Our boots slipped on the metal hulls coated with the harbor's bilge. We crested the gunnels, and laid down enough suppression fire to convince even the most heroic of the enemy to surrender. Just a few bloody examples were needed. Our first mission into the fray was a rout."

I soldiered on through my account. "The second front of our attack capturing the oil refineries went as smooth. It was a luxury not normally afforded irregular battalions such as ours. The Australians took their lumps capturing

Basra, while Father and I handled some wet work at the German officer's quarters in Khorramshar. The laundry hung out to dry and the ports captured, Operation Marmalade made our foothold in Iran by the summer's end. We bid our compatriots "Adieu" in Al's Bar, with a send-off worthy of dead heroes. It was the only place in all of Persia a soldier got legless drinking American whiskey. The next morning, we caught the first train north to Tehran on the Trans-Iranian Railway."

"Brilliant, mate," Angus chirped. "Brilliant. How was the food?"

"Nothing you wouldn't eat."

"Piss off. What was your next mission?" In the retelling, Angus's occasional questions echoed through the room, probing the depths of wartime experiences.

"Churchill gave us a checklist before we shipped out. Our first order task was securing the railway, which was paramount to the success of the new Russian Front. Father took coal and soil samples, while I drew the bridges and tunnels on a map. In the train station towns following the ancient Silk Road, we honored its history by sharing war plans here—and delivering ultimatums there. We traversed the tracks to the opposite ends of the railway, from Bandar Shahpour on the southern end to the northernmost station of Bandar Torkaman. We measured stream flow through gorges and waterfalls, and checked for structural cracks and enemy bombs on bridge abutments and tunnels.

"We received a message through a courier in Tehran we were finally to meet our Russian counterpart, Dimitry. He and his small platoon had been working on Nazi sympathizers to pass the time. Done with the daily rubbish, he met us in hopes of sharing our new climbing gear—a gift from George the Sixth.

"We marked him in the station by tells. The sleeves of his overcoat were rolled to his elbows. His black pahlavi hat sat on the bench beside him. His hands were in his pockets. When he recognized Father, he grabbed his hat, stood up, and covered his eyes under the short bill. We stood out with our pale complexions. When I caught a stare from the locals, I turned away in mock distraction. Dimitry and Father exchanged knowing glances, and we abandoned the traveling soldier's customary shake-down. Without certainty of Dmitry's origin, I was betting my life on the odds of Father and I against anyone. It'd paid off plenty before."

"Safer bet than a deposit at the Old Lady on Threadneedle Street," Angus growled, referring to the London Stock Exchange.

"Right-O, Angus!" I agreed. "Two of Dimitry's tribal squad walked toward a couple of Ural motorcycles outside. We, too, climbed in the sidecars of their comrades, motors rumbling. The hard looks of the drivers bore down on us. We climbed aboard the empty seats and rode away. The others in the platoon motored in behind us from side streets around the train station. Dimitry showed us the best paths of access around the bridges and tunnels corkscrewing through the Alborz Mountain Range, profiting from his secret northern arrival only a few months before. As part of the brokered alliance, we brought diffusing tools and mountaineering equipment. We trained together, ate together and slept together under the stars of the Arabian nights. Neither of us favored the other with small arms. Our rifles and ammunition were hardly reliable, and both our versions came from the last war.

"The newest weapons went to the European Front to test Nazi mettle. They replaced the guns left loaded on the evacuated beaches of Dunkirk. Our removed position in the mountains required our technological sacrifice. The British purse favored us enough spring-operated STEN guns to cobble together a couple of workable weapons. Our comrades patrolled with the confidence of a five-shot, bolt-action Mosin. Its accuracy among the mountain peaks fed us during the brutal cold of the North Iranian winter. They were better for hunting stag than killing advancing militia. For guarding bucolic bridges, we were undeterred by our inferior armament, and we were without question gun-heavy."

Angus hungered for the details, having missed the action. "Did you meet anyone like me over there?"

"That's a funny thing to ask. There was one." I flamed his interest and meandered toward the truth, but not close enough to incense him. "Soldiers with your gift are incredibly hard to come by, Angus."

"What was he like?" he asked with his bushy eyebrow raised.

"Her name was Hera, more stubborn than you. She was a warrant officer on loan from the Belgian Resistance."

A long pause. With Angus that always meant surprise. "Did she sleep with you?"

"Of course, mate. We bivouacked outside. It's colder along the Alborz than our snug and icy Exmoor."

"Good girl," Angus praised the idea of her.

I soldiered on through the story. "Our days began and ended with trekking the Alborz Range—and sometimes by motorcycle. We filled the middles hunting and rappelling down the masonry edges of enormous bridge abutments in river gorges. The real fighting was thousands of miles away in North Africa. It was Libya and Egypt that ground under the tank tracks of Rommel's Panzers. We acted as disinterested guards watching the trains roll north and south.

"One day, Father and I dangled from the Pol-e Piroozi's center arch. We swung quietly above the river's roar. The bridge's bottomless drop to the rapids faded away as we took in the snow-capped vistas above."

Slicing through my remembrance, Angus inquired, "And, Hera?"

"She was fearless and climbed like a mountain ram, just your type."

"Did you see any combat along the railway?"

"Not until we'd traveled north of Tehran. Even then, only small arms fire from retreating Germans and Iranian sympathizers. We were protecting a railway lifeline to the Russians, along with architectural masterpieces. The Shah didn't want to blow the bridges any more than we did. He built them. The Yanks sent munitions north to the Russian front. The Russians, using the emotional advantage over the Shah's nostalgia, railed troops south to invade his country.

"Then how did Father die?" Angus demanded, turning the conversation.

With a sigh, I submitted to Angus' right to know a truth I'd kept from him. "Secret operation," I said. "Codename:

Eureka. News began to reach our outpost as momentum turned back to the Allies in Egypt. Rommel was running out of steam—and oil. The British 8th Army dashed his supply line and his path of retreat. Hitler was reeling from his loss of the Egyptian stronghold. He then abandoned his agreement with Stalin and invaded Russia, exactly as Sir Winston had warned. Stalin was caught flat-footed, and sought a grand alliance with Churchill and Roosevelt. Roosevelt gladly included him in the plan. Sir Winston played along, having need of Stalin as the useful idiot.

"One snowy morning, a motorcycle rode through camp and stopped by the fire to speak to Dimitry. The rider pointed up the mountain, exchanged some Russian grunts and sped away. Dimitry gathered all our combatants together, and relayed the message. A package of unknown identity, shape or size, was chugging down the tracks and required safe passage to Tehran. His source also mentioned a few Nazi leftovers were stoking the locals with guns and promises of Jewish gold. We had to deploy to the Paron Bridge immediately. We hopped on our Urals and kick-cranked the motors into action, then drove down the rocky road out of camp. Our guns were loaded and oozing with oil.

"Approaching the Paron Bridge on the Talar River, the sun flamed the brick abutments. The enormous pedestals and arched caps supported the train tracks. Without this link to American machines, the Russian Army would die at the brutal hands of the Third Reich.

"Father and I clipped in to our rappelling harnesses near the center of the bridge. We slung the barrels of our STEN guns across our backs, and dropped down under the span. Hera preferred terra firma to free-roping and bar-reled down the mountain across the rocks near the bridge's edge. As our feet touched the ground, we looked up to see a couple of dodgy blokes in bed sheets on the rails above us. They didn't seem in a rush or aggressive, and it wasn't the first time we'd seen sheepherders or other drifters in the wilderness."

"I can sense it. You were unprepared," Angus commented. He got up and began pacing the perimeter of the cavernous room around my makeshift hospital bed.

I continued, "We unclipped our hip seats and collected our gear at the bottom of the ravine. Hera came running past us and went straight for it. Strapped across the inside edge of the giant pillar was a proper bomb—not like those Syrian finger-mashers. There were fresh footprints around the concrete pedestals. Bits and pieces of fuse lay in the dirt. Father and I noticed the blokes had left, and we heard the train whistle.

"We had little time. Father ordered me to dismantle the bomb from the bricks while he negotiated the rest of Dimitry's team down the hill."

Angus leaned in, curious, "How big was the bomb? Did Hera find anymore?"

"The biggest I'd seen. Three bombs of six plastic sticks each, linked by the fuse. I ordered Hera to patrol the rest of the pedestals. I cut the fuses at arm's length of the stick's ends, yanked the detonators, and ripped the bombs off the brick. The train was approaching. We heard it before we saw it. Stalin's shovel-nosed black train emerged from the forest and headed down the track.

"The last of Dimitry's squad descended from the hills and reached the canyon floor. I laid the bombs together on the ground and repacked the tools in my knapsack. As I was snapping the canvas shut, I looked up, and saw motion. The attack was coming. They must've been alerted by the bomb detonator's misfire. They came up the canyon saddle wearing sashes and daggers. I recognized a German SS officer from his gray uniform with a black collar. He shouted orders in Arabic from the rear as the robed mercenaries flooded up the worn path, zig-zagging between the rocks. I lost interest in their politics when the black holes of their German issued MG 34 machine gun barrels nested with their eyes. Their gunstocks were buried in their beards and jerked their chins in time with the bullet strikes landing in the canyon wall behind us. The ammo fed so fast the gun fire sounded like a mechanical zipper.

"I whipped the sling of my gun around my shoulder and fed bullets into the mob. Father ducked behind the concrete pedestal. He bent down before me and hoisted the bombs I'd retrieved over his shoulder. Dimitry screamed above the automatic fire and exploding dust. Father used the cut fuses of each bomb like a rope handle. He ordered his squad into support fire from the cover of the rocks dotting the gorge.

"Father reached in my pack and grabbed a couple of detonators and fuse igniters. Then he ordered me to gain higher ground. 'Go fight from the rocks with Dimitry, Nick, and save me some bullets for this bloody STEN gun', he yelled. 'We'll finish these rogues off proper, mate.'"

"Where was Hera? Checking the bridge pedestals?" Angus asked.

"She came whipping around me just as I clocked the SS officer at the end of a trail of bullets. My gun overheated and the spring jammed. I slammed it to the ground in disgust and it fired one into the wind. War pissed, I looked up to see Father running toward the advancing Bedouins with the wrapped sticks of dynamite flailing across his back.

"Hera led me to another bundle of plastic explosives. Just then, a bullet smacked the bridge abutment above us. Both of us ducked as we were covered in mortar dust. In my side view, two of the Russian squad got hit. They snapped backward and fell to the bottom of the gorge, run through with bullet holes.

"I moved several yards down the jagged mountain slope, maneuvering behind the giant boulders. Father positioned himself above the chokepoint of their offensive. Dimitry's squad found targets, but their single-shot Mosins mostly splattered on the rocks around Father.

"Above the sounds of battle, the whistle of Stalin's train bled out, signaling its arrival. It crested the edge of the bridge on the high butte above us. The long black package, no longer a secret, chugged down the track right through the middle of our battle.

"The Marxist dictator," Angus asked, confused? "Why waste your lives on one no better than Hitler?"

"He was enroute to parlay with Roosevelt and Churchill in Tehran. The first-ever face-to-face meeting of the Allied Powers. It had the potential to end years of war."

"I should have been there," Angus howled. "Why did you leave me here? I am not human. I never was. So why do you keep expecting me to act like one? My breed is loyal, not lonely and subdued. You should have killed me before you left," he said. A long pause. Drained from the confession he'd buried deep, Angus collected himself. Finally, "Where was Hera?"

"There was nothing you could have done, Angus," I said tearfully, consoling him. "In all the action, I lost sight of her until I saw her following Father down the canyon between the boulders. He'd gotten so close to the attackers that he looked like one of them. Hera by his side, Father tossed the three bombs high above the chokepoint where the approaching militia were converged. The explosion burst directly above them, decimating everything under the blast. Father and Hera were gone. It was a valiant end. Their deaths likely saved millions.

"The bottom of the bridge blocked my view of the train, but the smoke boiling from the smokestack was almost above me. I had no time to pull my tools from the knapsack, so I ripped the last bomb from the bridge masonry and flung it high above the Bedouins coming from my left. The smoldering fuse lifted off the ground. The sparks vanished and ignited a blast at the center of my toss. The vibrating masonry and the train whistle were the last thing I remember." The weight of the memory jolted my soul. My toes wiggled, and my mouth opened.

For the first time in weeks, my eyes cracked into slits. The room was silent. The story faded as the smell of books filled my nose. Mother was still at rest in her faraway dreams. Angus licked her face, stirring her awake. Angus came over and put his paws on my chest and began licking my cheek. Mother came to me. She looked in my eyes, put her hands to her face, and began to cry. "Angus," she blubbered, "get down. He's been in a coma for God's sake. Oh, thank God you're back, Nicholas. Thank God." She ran to the door, flung it open, and yelled, "Elle, get the doctor! Nicholas is awake! He's awake!"

I grabbed Angus by his furry neck and rolled it while he licked my face. "Hello, ole' boy. Thanks for the lift." I laid in a warm cocoon, surrounded by shelves and shelves of great old stories. The library held the ancient secrets of dynasties past, and the family narrative, as we awaited the next chapter in the Thorne legacy. A bomb explosion from His Majesty's testing range rattled the chandeliers, shocking me into the present and calling me back to the fight.

www.ingramcontent.com/pod-product-compliance
Lightning Source LLC
Chambersburg PA
CBHW020327200626
46814CB00006BB/2452